Halogen Nig

and Other Love St

MW01167397

Foreword

by Ken Liu

With the work of an author worth reading, you have to be prepared to learn a new language. Good writers do not write in some generic grapholect such as "Modern Standard American English" whose primary purpose is commerce, instruction, the conformity of individual expression to convention and cliché in the interest of "efficiency of communication"; rather, they invent a new tongue, with its own syntax and vocabulary, its own rhythm and prosody, uniquely suited to give you a flavor of their mind, to stretch your senses into new dimensions, to tell you stories that only they can tell.

Think of Faulkner, Hemingway, Woolf, Hughes, Stein, Morrison, Nabokov, Le Guin ... How immediately identifiable each voice is! You could pick out the author sometimes based on a single line. They had to invent their own words, images, syntaxes, and languages to make you see the world the way they want you to see it, and you were glad to learn to speak their tongues.

I've known Anatoly Belilovsky's writing from the very beginning of his literary career—when we were both baby writers, still trying to figure out what stories we wanted to tell, still striving to invent the new languages to tell them in. Tolya and I were critique partners who met through an online workshop. Even then, I could see that the language he was crafting was going to thrum with power: multilingual puns, cosmopolitan allusions, scientific terminology artfully repurposed as kennings; ornate sentences that reformed the syntax of English into Klein bottles; the macabre and the nostalgic placed side by side in a brutal collage brimming with tenderness; history redeemed through the courage to laugh and mock those in power.

I knew right away I was in the presence of a grand soul and a fantastic writer. I know now also that I have been blessed with a wonderful friend.

Over time, I've watched in awe as he has grown ever more confident in the crafting of his language, elaborating it, evolving it, proliferating it and then pruning it ... until he has the perfect language needed to tell the stories that he wants to tell. Few writers have the skill and the determination to get this far. We readers are lucky to have him.

Be prepared to learn a new language. Be prepared to see the universe anew.

Ken Liu is the author of *The Grace of Kings* and *The Paper Menagerie and Other Stories*.

Halogen Nightmares

The first thing they tell you is, no one has come back yet. This in itself isn't surprising, but the way the recruiting officer says it, it seems like they don't expect anyone back, ever. I hear intakes of breath around me, but there is no sense of movement. The room is pitch black; if I leave now, no one will see my shame. No one but me.

That night I dream of fluorine.

Fluorine has killed, or tried to kill, every chemist who tried to isolate it. Water burns in fluorine. So does asbestos. Fluorinated superacids dissolve paraffin, glass, platinum. Fluorine burns are insidious, taking hours to manifest, and also very difficult to treat.

My fluorine dreams are of burning: of launch pad fire like Apollo 1, of midair explosion like Challenger, or heat shield failure like Columbia; electric fire, heat shield failure, straying too near the Sun.

In this one I walk barefoot on boiling molten metal. Dream pain is a remote sensation but the sight of flesh melting off the bones fascinates me. In the dream I know the name of each bone I see, and I name them out loud before they too disintegrate, one by one, and I sink lower. Dream logic tells me I am not dead until my eyes descend into the liquid fire, and when they do, the dream allows me to die and so wake up.

I take my shower as cold as I can stand, and wait as long as possible before I put on clothes to report to breakfast.

The second day they put you in a mockup fighter cockpit and leave you there, alone, in pitch dark again. The cockpit springs open if you make a noise louder than a whisper, or push something in it too hard. The windshield is inches from your nose, side hatches brush your shoulders, roof close enough to ruffle your hair when you turn your head. If they sense your fear, they take you out and bring you home.

You are allowed to sleep; encouraged, even. This is a test of nerves, not endurance. That comes later. The first hour I hear others sob, call out for help; then it's quiet. I didn't sleep well the night before, and so I drift off, fitfully, and dream of chlorine.

Chlorine was the first halogen discovered, and is still the most abundant and easiest to isolate. During World War One it was used as a poison gas. It caused edema of the lungs.

The chlorine nightmares are of suffocation: suit failure on EVA, cabin depressurization like Soyuz 11, running out of stored oxygen. In this one I am crawling through a tunnel, trying to escape from something I cannot see. I know it to be horrible; so horrible that, as tunnel narrows and as breathing gets more difficult by the second, I keep on going till --

I wake up in my bunk, sit up, and give myself over to the ecstasy of breathing.

The third day there are considerably fewer of us in the room. The folding chairs are replaced with chaise lounges; sounds of rain and surf emanate from hidden speakers. We are given mathematical problems to solve. Drill instructors walk softly among us. They write down names of those who fall asleep.

Bromine is less common than chlorine, and less reactive. As the bromide salt, it was once used as a sedative.

The bromine nightmare is of giving up: of watching aliens' missiles approach, of having point defense systems control, of thinking: why bother? Why postpone the inevitable? Everyone dies. Now is as good a time as ever.

When it's too late to change my mind I hear my mother's voice behind me. She's calling me to dinner. I turn and see the house I grew up in, my parents, my sister, my best friend, both boys I liked in junior high. I reach for the control board knowing I'll never launch countermeasures in time, and wake up.

The five of us who are still here are naked in a room. The door is locked with five combination locks, each labeled with our names and personal questions: grandmother's birthday, last four digits of Global ID, score of the last basketball game you played in high school. The answer unlocks that one lock.

Two DIs have fire hoses going full blast. The only way for each of us to unlock their own lock is to have all the others form a human shield between them and the hoses.

We are done in two minutes flat.

Iodine is a solid, also the heaviest stable halogen. The body traps iodine in the thyroid gland, where it is used in the synthesis of thyroid hormones. Radionuclide studies have shown that iodine stays in the body for years.

Iodine at room temperature is a purple–black solid, both volatile and crystalline.

The iodine nightmare is of her hurtling through the darkness of space beyond the orbit of Mars, solar cells degraded or fractured or misoriented, caesium cold and useless without power for the Hall Effect thruster.

I don't know what the astatine nightmares are. There are no stable isotopes of astatine; all decay with half–lives on the order of hours at the most, seconds to minutes for the most part. The astatine nightmares wake me, sweating, from sleep, linger briefly, and disperse in the morning light.

Some astatine isotopes undergo alpha decay. The alpha particle is the nucleus of helium, a noble gas.

Noble gases also include neon, argon, xenon, krypton, and radon. Noble gases are known for their reluctance to form molecules. All noble gas nightmares are the same.

They are all about being alone.

Pas de Deux

Monday:

The narrow corridor got stuffier as the seconds ticked off. Kevin's sweat beaded on his forehead, stained the back of his shirt. Valerie leaned against the wall, away from Kevin.

"It's not working," he whispered. "You sure it's the right door?"

Valerie crouched. "Reach up and feel the nameplate," she whispered. "Feel the letters. What are they?"

He lifted his hand, patted the door, stopped. "Umm, OK, feels like C, O, then something... then another O..."

"Connors Demolitions, as advertised," she whispered. "Now, back to work. Remember what I told you. Nice and easy. One pin at a time. Can you tell which ones feel springy?"

"I think so," Kevin whispered.

"And the clicks when they set?"

"Yeah. Yeah, here's one!"

"You're doing fine. Keep constant tension on the pick, don't try to force it," she whispered.

Footsteps echoed through the building.

"Shit," Kevin whispered. "Is that a guard?"

"I'll take care of him," Valerie whispered. "You concentrate on that lock. After it opens--"

"Detonators are in the cigar box in the top right desk drawer," Kevin whispered. "I remember." She heard him swallow, smacking his dry lips. "What... what are you going to do with him?"

"The guard?" she said. "Why do you want to know?"

"Well..." He paused, straightened his back. "Umm..."

"You wanted to strike a blow for Mother Gaia, didn't you?" she said.

"Umm... yeah?" he whispered and stared over Valerie's head.

"Second thoughts?" she said.

"Umm... no?" he said, his voice quivering.

She rose from her crouch, pirouetted in silence, and tip-toed down the corridor toward the guard's desk. It was Larry's turn on night duty, you could always count on Larry's prostate to send him to the can every half-hour like clockwork. That, and a cigarette at quarter-to and quarter-past.

She could almost taste the smoke of Larry's cigarette as she walked toward him. Bumming a cigarette off Larry was never a problem.

Tuesday:

Kevin's hand shook as he poured nitric acid into the glass bowl. The mixture seethed, an orange mist rising above it.

"You sure this is safe?" he said, his voice muffled by his respirator.

"I hope so," Valerie answered.

Kevin's hand drew back. "What do you mean, you hope so?" He turned to Valerie, his expression hidden by his goggles.

"I hope you did a thorough job, washing all that glassware," she said. "TNT is a pussycat if it's pure. If you left any dirt in there, we'll have pockets of unreacted dinitrotoluene, and that stuff will detonate if you look at it crosseyed."

Kevin took a breath and resumed pouring.

"Where'd you learn all that?" he asked.

"Premed," she said, and turned away to hide a smile.

Wednesday:

"How much farther?" Kevin gasped.

"Two miles," Valerie answered. "And lose that scared-shitless look. If anyone sees us, we're hikers."

"With enough explosives to blow up a small town," Kevin said.

"You did remember to put the detonators in your pockets, right?" Valerie said.

"Yeah," Kevin said.

"You sure?" Valerie said. "'Cause if you fall down, and they go off in a backpack full of TNT..."

"I'm sure," Kevin hissed between his teeth.

Thursday:

"We could have done this yesterday," Kevin said. He slapped a putty-like blob onto a girder and reached into his pocket.

"STOP!" Valerie bellowed. "What did I tell you? Set all the charges first, then go back and attach all the detonators. You're making mistakes, and that's after a good night's rest. If I was tired, too, I might not catch them all. Now, take another charge of TNT and put it --" she pointed to a girder junction farther up "-- there."

"Shit," Kevin said. "I gotta climb that?"

"You gotta climb that," Valerie said.

He pulled himself up, his feet scrambling for a ledge. "We'll set it off tonight?"

"Tomorrow morning," she said.

"Be warmer if we shared a sleeping bag," he said.

She sighed. It never failed. Sooner or later, they all got around to *that*.

"I won't be sleeping," she said. "Gotta check placement one more time." *And this time, use real plastique with real detonators*, she added silently.

He sighed and resumed climbing.

Friday:

"Now?" Kevin said.

Valerie nodded. Kevin pushed the plunger.

The flash seemed too small, as did the cloud that rose in silence from the base of the transmission tower. Kevin's face quirked.

"That's--" he began.

The wall of sound hit them then, a palpable avalanche of roar and thunder, slamming air from Kevin's chest and plastering his face with clumps of topsoil. He jumped to his feet, tearing off his goggles, spitting the dirt jammed in his mouth. In the distance, the tower listed slowly, then gathered speed and fell, another cloud of dust rising at its impact.

"Boo-yah!" Kevin shouted, and danced a clumsy jig. "Take that, imperialist polluter bastard pigs! Strike a blow for a green Earth!"

Valerie applauded with all the sincerity she could muster.

Saturday:

There was an email from Connors in her inbox:

"Well done! I don't know how you manage to low-ball, but it isn't by cutting corners. I have another job next month: Williston Electric just completed their wind farm; they need the old smokestack taken down. I hope you bid."

Sunday:

Her phone rang. She picked it up.

"Hi," the voice on the phone said. "It's Kevin."

"Kevin, listen," she said, "I asked you not to call – _"

"Just wanted to thank you," he said.

"Think you got your money's worth?" she said.

"You kidding?" he said. "Can't wait to tell the guys at work tomorrow. Best. Vacation. *Ever!*"

Hither and Yon

"So how'd you guys get together?" Katie asked.

We stopped at the top of the rise, leaned against a pink wall in the shade of an awning: Janie and I, and the couple we met at dinner, first night of the cruise. It was an effort to remember their names: Katie and Kevin. I kept thinking of them as Lucy and Ralph. As in, Ricardo and Kramden.

"George and I met at a Cancellation Day party," said Janie.

For a moment I flashed on Janie as I saw that day, gift-wrapped in black tights and a golden tunic.

"A whosie-whatsit day party?" said Kevin.

"June 3, 2009." I said. "40 years to the day since 'Turnabout Intruder' aired. The final episode. Janie came dressed as Kirk."

I looked at Janie, and she at me, and once again my breath caught. Our eyes had met that day through the dry ice fog that poured from a punch bowl; hers were set to stun. A smile pulled my cheeks like a tipsy great-aunt at a wedding rehearsal.

"And you went on a cruise for your second anniversary," said Kate. "How romantic! I bet he never forgets your anniversary, like you do, half the time, right, Kevin?"

"I thought Kirk was a man," Kevin said.

"He was," Janie answered. "Except in that episode, he gets body-swapped. I borrowed a command tunic –" She squared her shoulders.

"You musta looked hot," said Kevin.

"Don't go changing the subject," said Kate. "We were talking about how thoughtless you are."

"Once," Kevin muttered. "I forgot it once."

"Right," said Kate. "I can count. You forgot *our* second anniversary, that's one out of two. Half the time."

Kevin took a breath to say something, thought better of it, and deflated in silence. Janie did the eyebrow shrug, Vulcan style. I looked around, anywhere but at Kate and Kevin.

We turned and walked toward the Hamilton wharf under a long awning shared by a dozen tiny storefronts. The air grew cooler as an onshore breeze swirled dust and fallen leaves in pirouettes and loops; a cloud drew across the sun, tempering its glare with the mercy of shade.

"Oooh, look at these!" said Kate, her all-penetrating voice now coming from the other side of the street. "Janie, come over here!"

"What time is it?" said Janie. "I think it's getting late..." The last word sounded Dopplered-down.

I turned to look. Kate had a hold on Janie's hand and one foot in the doorway of a shoe store on the other side of the street.

"Hurry up, Kate!" yelled Kevin from behind me. "We got a ship to catch!"

Janie flashed me a come-hither look: come-hither and save me, that is.

"*--I'll protect you, fair maiden!*" I shouted.

"*--Sorry, neither!*" she shouted back.

"Huh?" Katie said, her head tilted.

"The Naked Time," Janie said.

Janie loved being rescued. She'd never actually *needed* to be saved, until now. I turned to follow, but with one last yank Kate pulled Janie through the doorway, and the door slammed shut.

Kevin grinned, not unsympathetically. He straightened his back and began to whistle a familiar tune. The words came to me as if he spoke them:

"Hello, silence, my old friend,

I've come to talk to you again..."

A flash of lightning answered him.

In seconds, the sky darkened and began to churn; thunder rolled over us as air tingled with ozone. I started across the street. It wasn't that wide; a few drops of rain weren't going to stop me.

I would have made it, too, most places. Not in Bermuda.

Halfway across, lightning and thunder hit me in a single body blow, and rain roared in my face like a rabid fire hose. Next thing I knew, Kevin was pulling me up and back under the awning, both of us soaking wet.

"Jeez," said Kevin. I barely heard him, between the downpour and the ringing in my ears. "Thought you was a goner there for a second. Close call!"

I scrambled up. Beyond the awning there was only a wall of rain.

"But..." I said. "The girls..."

"I'm sure the shoe store is still there," said Kevin.

"We can't just leave them," I said.

"They probably didn't even notice," he said. "We'll wait here. Boat's not going to leave without us. Maybe we can go inside someplace..."

"But..." I shook water out of my hair, wiped my eyes. The rain, if anything, got stronger. I backed away from the spray off the awning, as if it could have got me any wetter.

"Hey, check this out!" said Kevin, pointing behind me. "It's a video store! Let's go look!"

I followed Kevin through the glass door. It closed behind us, muffling the rain to a whisper. An ancient air conditioner wheezed and rattled overhead; flyspecked lights flickered from murk to gloom and back again. We dripped on the doormat.

"Let's just stay here," I said. "I don't want to leave the place a mudbath."

"Come on in," said a muffled voice from farther inside. Kevin raised an eyebrow at me. I shrugged.

We advanced a step. Kevin flicked the last of the rain from his eyes, stared at the stack in front of him. Several rows of very pretty couples stared back.

"Would you get a load of that?" said Kevin. "Chick flicks. A wall of chick flicks. Not one movie I ever heard of. Or wanted to. I tell you, everything is for chicks these days. Chick flicks, chick shops, chick clubs. I bet a chick runs this..."

A tall bearded man, aged anything from thirty to sixty, came out from behind the stack. He walked with a stork's high-stepping gait; in his tilted face owl's eyes blinked, magnified by thick round glasses.

"Can I help you with anything?" He said, in a voice that would have been Bela Lugosi's if Bela Lugosi had been a Texan.

Kevin and I traded a look again.

"You are welcome to sit out the rain," he added, blinking.

Kevin blinked back at him. "Sci-fi," he said. "My friend here likes sci-fi."

I cringed.

"*SF* is in the corner," said the proprietor, sounding like an English butler played by a Texan Bela Lugosi. "Here, let me show you."

"Whassamatta with you, George?" Kevin hissed. "Can't you see? He's busting your chops. Yanking your chain. Jerking you--"

"I get your point," I said.

"So let's call him on it," Kevin whispered. "Give him the fifty bucks and tell him to put on the show, right here, right now. I betcha he'll say the player is busted." He pointed at a TV-DVD combo behind the counter. "I swear I'll punch him out if he does that."

I looked at the shelf. The boxes were still there. Nice shiny shrink-wrapped boxes, about the right size for DVDs, with genuine-looking iridescent lettering: *STAR TREK: SEASONS 1-5, STARFLEET JAG, STAR TREK: VULCAN ACADEMY, STAR TREK: MIDSHIPMEN.* Some of the credits brought tears to my eyes, others made my mouth water; each sang to me its sweet siren song. *"Script by Philip K. Dick." "Directed by John Carpenter." "Guest stars: Marlon Brando, Bette Davis."* I looked at the proprietor. He looked back, blinking. I looked out the window.

The wind picked that particular moment to fling a sheet or ten of rain at the plate-glass window, turning the street outside into a mess of funhouse mirrors. Such a small decision: Kevin and I walked down one side of the street, Kate and Janie on the other, men ducking left, women right. *Mirror, Mirror...*

Kevin was probably right. It was a hoax, had to be. There are no gateways between universes. Not even in Bermuda.

"Well?" Kevin asked.

"It would be," murmured a silent inner voice, raising one eyebrow, *"a highly illogical assumption. The odds against it are − astronomical."*

A minuscule, tiny, infinitesimal risk.

"Bermuda Triangle? It's a myth! A tale to frighten children!" another voice snapped. *"Dammit, I'm a doctor, not a folklorist!"*

"George?" said Kevin. "Hello?"

"No," I said firmly.

"'No I don't want to make a fool out of this jerk,' or 'No I don't want to see the final episode of Star Trek by'--who did you say it was?"

"Frank Herbert," I answered automatically. "Or so he says." I nodded at the salesman. The salesman grinned, tilting his head even more.

"So which is it?" Kevin demanded. He shook stray raindrops from his nose with a sideways jerk. He would have looked like a rooster if roosters looked like fireplugs.

"No, I don't want to take a chance of losing Janie," I said slowly.

Kevin threw up his hands. "Can you believe this guy?" he asked of no one in particular.

The proprietor fielded the question himself. "I haven't believed either of you guys since you opened your mouths," he said. "You are either senile or Canadian, is what I think. Best TV show of all time, canceled after three seasons?" he continued. "President Heinlein would have flown us Marines out of Hanoi to take over the studio if they tried that. I wish he'd done that, I was gettin' bored babysitting Giap."

I ran for the door, Kevin a breath behind me.

Rain squalls don't last long in Bermuda, which is just as well. You will hardly ever be late for anything if you wait one out. I did not wait. I ran into and through the curtain of warm water, slipping on bumps and splashing through puddles, until I felt a solid wall against my hands.

I wiped my eyes. By sheer dumb luck, I stood against the window of the shoe store I'd seen Janie go into. I saw Kate right away, turning a slipper this way and that inches in front of her face. It took the longest second of my life to find Janie, talking with a salesgirl in the dark interior of the shop.

"Any other day," Kevin growled behind me, "I'd'a said you've been out in the sun too long." He pushed open the door and shoved me into the shoe store.

"Give me a break," I said.

"I can do that, George," Kevin said, more Brooklyn than usual in his voice. "You want a break to your face or a break to your kneecap?"

"And that's why we are standing here making puddles of ourselves," Kevin concluded.

"Wow," said Kate. "This is so romantic. Kevin, would you ever do something like that for me?"

"I'm standing here dripping, don't I?" he said. "Braved the elements, and all that."

"It's not the same," said Kate.

"How is it not the same?" Kevin roared. "We ran the same, we got wet the same--"

"George had a more romantic reason," Kate declared. "Even if I don't understand it."

"Schroedinger's cat?" Janie asked.

I nodded. "Exactly."

"What?" Kevin said.

"One possible explanation for the Bermuda Triangle," I said, "is the Many Worlds hypothesis, itself a corollary of Schroedinger's thought experiment--"

"Please, George. English," Kevin said.

"Short version?" I said. "If this is true, then, I thought, watching the videos from an alternate reality would collapse the wave function in that reality. We'd have to stay there."

"And what would be wrong with that?" Kevin demanded. "Five seasons of Star Trek. Winning the Vietnam War. Or do you think that would have been bad, winning the war?"

"Screw the war," I said. "Janie and I wouldn't be together."

"Why not?" Kate broke in. "I always thought you two were destined for each other. A perfect couple. Why can't we be like them, Kevin?"

Kevin took a breath to answer. Janie beat him to it.

"We would have had no reason," she said, "to meet that day."

"Two years, two days ago," I said. "If that weren't Cancellation Day, neither of us would have gone to ConTrek. No cancellation, no party."

"Ooh, goosebumps!" said Kate. "Hey! Rain's gone. Let's go over there again."

"Sure," said Kevin. "Maybe we'll collapse into a reality where I never forgot anything. Or where you learned to keep your mouth shut."

"You're such a pig, Kevin," said Kate. "If you made your own universe, all the women in it would be barefoot and pregnant."

"Not really. They'd be bare-butt and--" Kevin began.

"Bare-butt and pliable?" I suggested.

"Bare-bust and programmable," Janie said.

"Season Five?" The proprietor took off his glasses. "What planet are you guys from?"

"Told ya he was yanking your chain," Kevin said. "Let's go, Kate. Back to the ship, it's sailing in an hour."

"Everybody knows there wasn't but *one* season of Trek," the salesman continued, in the same Texan Bela Lugosi voice.

Janie started to walk toward the door. Kevin and I followed.

"A short one, too, only twelve episodes," the salesman continued. "I guess America wasn't ready for a woman Number One."

I stumbled, caught myself. Janie took my hand. We walked on, toward the open door.

"Some say, though," he said, "it was the show that helped get President Bush elected."

"Bush?" said Kate. She walked just behind Kevin, holding his hand. "What's *he* got to do with it?"

The salesman laughed. "*He?* What are you guys, Canadian? Everybody knows there's but one brain in *that* family, and that's Barbara."

Janie froze in the doorway. I tried to stop but slipped in my own puddle. Newton's Laws seemed to work the same in this universe as anywhere else; the hundred pounds or so I have on Janie swept us both out the door. I grabbed at an awning support to keep from falling. My momentum spun me to face the door as I clung on.

Kevin's face was only visible for a second; I saw what had to be Kate's hand on his shoulder, fingers dug deep into the folds of his shirt. After his face receded into the dark interior of the store, slipping from sight like a drowning man's, a lightning flashed, and seared on my retina his very last look.

When we came back into the store, we found no one there but the same proprietor: stork-gaited, owl-eyed. And on the shelves, the three familiar seasons of *STAR TREK TOS*, plus the expected *TNG*, *Voyager*, and movies. No surprises in the credits: Ted Sturgeon, Harlan Ellison, Ricardo Montalban. I looked at Janie; she looked at me and took my hand. We left without a word, and walked together to the pier, touching more and talking less than ever before.

Someone else had Kate's and Kevin's cabin on the cruise ship; the strangers had been there since sailing from New York. Another couple had their places at the late dinner seating. Even the memories are fading, though Kate's glass-on-Styrofoam voice might haunt me for a while. The last I'll probably remember of Kevin, like a Cheshire cat's smile, might be that desperate last look.

The "come-hither" look.

The "come hither and save me" look.

Last Man Standing

Mother died today, or maybe it was yesterday; I wasn't there to notice. I brought her a jar of moonshine for breakfast, same as always, and her bed was empty. No way she could have walked off if she was still Mom, not all torn up from the zombie attack, so she had to have died and gone to join them.

Could have been worse. *I* could have been her breakfast. Or mid-rats. Depending on when she's passed.

Funny word, mid-rats. Dad told me once it meant mid-watch rations, bug juice and sandwiches in the middle of the night in Navy talk, but I always imagined sailors gnawing on skewered rats. It was good for a giggle when there wasn't much else to laugh about. Not with Mom converting Dad's pension into liquid assets: moonshine so raw it sat you on your ass just to smell it. Not with Child Welfare looking to take me away. I could not have stopped them from taking Mom if they wanted to; but wasn't nobody going to take me. Not from <u>my</u> house. If they had taken me from my bedroom, from Mom's kitchen, from Dad's garage, from the beans and the potatoes growing near-wild and the chickens running 'round, from the sweet gum logs in the woodpile and the woods out back, slimecap mushrooms poking out from between dead leaves and itchy-balls in the fall, and Blackjack and Bear, two yellow dogs too old to hunt and too smart to bark – who am I without all of that?

And then the zombies came.

I don't know where they came from; lots of people say they do, and they all say different. I just know they promised immortality, and I said to Mom, wouldn't that be great, Dad would still be alive, and you wouldn't ever be dead, and she looked away and chugged what 'shine was left in the jar and tottered off to sleep. And I sat up and looked at the moon and listened to the possums rummage in the junk pile and pretty soon I saw Dad again. I'd fallen asleep on a haystack, and in my dream I ran to him to tell him he'd be back home soon, and he just shook his head and sighed and said, "Son, I don't think immortality is retroactive," and I woke up to rooster crowing and the sky across the road pinking up just a little, though it was black and starry overhead.

I never brought up immortality again till zombies started showing up.

They are immortal, those zombies, and they carry the infection that makes you immortal – or damn near, barring shotgun blast to the head or getting burned to cinders. They all look young and pretty; that, and they don't feel pain or cold so they've let their clothes fall apart on them – ones that still have shreds clinging to them look nakeder than the ones that don't, which, when I thought about it, is a bigger temptation than immortality, and I probably would not ever have said "No" to them if they took "No" for an answer.

Which they don't.

They come at you with this great big smile and they try their damnedest to bite you.

Just like the child welfare people, except for the biting part, and the part with no clothes, but the smile is the same and so is the not asking if you want to do what they've come to get done, and the part where they tell you it's for your own good.

They came last night, and Mom took one look at me and one at them and took a swig of shine and said, "run, boy!" and charged them with a hoe that she picked up off the floor, that had been there since she shook it at the child welfare people, and I ran for the woods which I still knew better than anyone, and Blackjack and Bear took off, barking, in damn near the opposite direction. Them are two smart yellow dogs. And I came back to find Mom all bit and bruised and running a fever and put her to bed, and saved one jar of 'shine for if she was still here in the morning, as Mom I mean, and not a thing that walks when Mom is gone, and poured the rest of the 'shine on the floor to cover puddles of zombie blood, 'cause that's contagious, too, I guess, and I don't want to step in it, getting up at oh-dark-hundred one night, and turn into a zombie by accident.

No graves to visit: Dad lost at sea, Mom found life everlasting. Preachers made that sound so good, back when there were churches. Mom never came back; none ever do. None ever try to bite their own. I guess you don't need immortality through your kin when you can have it through not dying. Why do they spend eternity just wandering around? Guess they should have asked the aliens that, first, before climbing on board the No-Death Express.

The dogs came back, just like I knew they would. I wouldn't mind *them* living forever, but the infection don't work that way. I'll be here for as long as I can, and when the time comes, I'll go. I wonder if I can go to heaven. Heaven is where Mom picks eggs from under the chickens and fries them up with onions and bacon and tomatoes, and Dad's feet stick out from under the rusted Chevy when he's on leave, and Blackjack and Bear fly past you like two yellow streaks, yipping and panting. Heaven is where my family is.

I don't want to go to Hell. Hell is other people.

The Perils of Bonaparte

August 18, 1812

Dearest Josephine,

Smolensk is hot, dusty and oppressive. Russian opposition was light, the bulk of their army withdrew as soon as they saw Prince Poniatowski's uhlans put spurs to their mounts, there was some trifling action at the city walls, and Murat's corps entered on the heels of the Vistula Legion having hardly smelled any smoke. The city is burned out, of course, and there is little food. We found a cauldron of groats in an intact corner of one building; a bit insipid but somewhat palatable.

In the distance, in the encampment of the Russian rear guard, Prince Bagration's soldiers are singing something that to my ear clearly appears written by men who eat Russian groats all day. It is insipid and mildly nauseating, but in its own way melodic, and how can I ever again cringe at a musical piece after having heard the braying of Egyptian camels?

Onward, and--*l'audace! Toujours l'audace!*

Napoleon

September 7, 1812

Here at Borodino, the Russians are dug in and well equipped; their songs sound rather worse with full orchestration than sung a capella. Poor Caulaincourt keeled over of apoplexy almost immediately, and several of my officers appeared greenish around the gills, but then our men discharged their first musket salvo which drowned out the music in a most satisfactory manner, and thereafter reloaded their muskets with rapidity I had never before seen, or believed possible. I shall ascribe that to their finer musical sensibilities--or perhaps to olfactory ones, as the brimstone constituent of gunpowder smoke provided an effective anodyne for the odour of groats emanating from Russian dugouts.

I am told the songs are all written by a man named Ilya Krivoy. I have ordered him caught and shot. *A la guerre comme a la guerre!*

September 14, 1812
We arrived at Moscow in the evening. The only significant opposition came from a peasant wedding that spilled out of a church in Borisovka, a village just outside the city: these abominable songs accompanied by accordion and balalaika appear to hit the exact pitch required to set French teeth on edge; the sequences of notes repeated ad nauseam reminded one of being sliced in half with a two-handed saw, forever. Two hundred soldiers and three officers were sickened, but are expected to recover in a few weeks, and as soon as our cannon caught up, a dozen canister shot eliminated this annoyance.

I have announced a reward of ten roubles for capture of Krivoy, alive or dead. I intend to execute him publicly. They have their songs and I have my smoothbores; we'll see which has *plus bang de son franc.*

September 15, 1812

The fire of Moscow begins. We caught some 400 arsonists, all of whom sang as they set the city aflame. All claimed to be working under orders. I had them all shot, and buried in a forest. Let their friends wander about looking for them, *a la recherche de tombes perdu.*

October 18, 1812

It seems all the Russians left in Moscow are eating groats and singing songs. Is there no humanity left to them? I raised the reward for Krivoy to twenty roubles dead or one hundred roubles alive; a rouble nowadays buys either three tonnes of groats, or half a chicken. I spend much time plotting an appropriate demise for this Krivoy, assuming I buy the more expensive package of him. I also ordered summary executions on the spot for anyone caught singing, copying sheet music, or in possession of a balalaika, *pour décourager les autres.*

November 20, 1812

I have driven all remaining Russians from Moscow; it seemed the only way, short of shooting the lot, of stopping the excruciating vocalizations, each melody like a garrotte constricting around one's unmentionables. I confiscated all their food, of course, except for the abominable groats; they protest, *et j'agite mes partes intimes a leurs tantes.*

November 21, 1812
QUEL HORREUR!
At night, Moscow is filled with wolves!
Howling wolves!
Wolves howling Krivoy's songs in four part harmony!
Run away!
Sauve qui peut!

Durak

"Is dangerous, this ice," said the Russian.

The great frozen mass approached slowly, the steward struggling to push the cart across the threshold of the card room.

"I agree," said the New Yorker. He shuffled a deck of cards, rather listlessly. "Looks like it's about to give our steward here a hernia."

"I only wanted enough to put in my brandy," said the Texan. "Why'd he bring the whole brick?"

"White Star line is very prideful of her service," said the steward.

"They don't do anything small on the Titanic," the New Yorker said. "Not in first class, anyway."

The steward brought down the icepick with a practiced stroke. Shards of ice fell, glittering, on the plate. The steward dropped them into the Texan's glass.

"The danger right now," the Englishman said, "is that a Frenchman might walk in. He would be well within his rights to shoot you for this sacrilege. Ice in Armagnac--"

"It's just brandy," the Texan said. "You ain't French, are you, boy?"

"No, Sir," the steward replied.

"That's a funny accent," said the Texan. "Where're you from?"

"Transylvania," said the steward. "Sir."

"Quinsy," said the Russian. "You could make cold your throat and die of quinsy. Is what happened to your George Washington. He die of quinsy." The Russian paused. "In December. When is cold."

"He died of bloodletting," said the New Yorker.

"In America they use bloodletting?" said the Russian. "In Russia we use leeches. Nobody die of leeches. What they use in England?"

"Transylvanians," the Englishman said.

"What?" the Russian said.

"Will there be anything else?" the steward said.

"No," the Russian said. "Transylvanians for leeches?"

"Vampires," the Englishman said.

"Ah," the Russian said. "From Mr. Stoker's book. Is funny."

"You read Dracula?" the New Yorker said.

"I read all English books," said the Russian. "Sherlock Houses. Brave Captains. Machine of the Times."

"H. G. Wells!" the Englishman exclaimed. "You like Wells!"

"I read Wells," said the Russian. "I not like Wells."

"I can't stand Wells, either. Damned Socialist," The Texan said.

"I rather liked War of the Worlds, myself," said the New Yorker. "In the end, when the invaders die of influenza – "

"Could I fetch more ice?" the steward said.

"We've plenty," the Texan said. "What Wells wrote -- that's just damn fool nonsense. Can't happen."

"Why not?" the Englishman asked.

"First of all, down on the ranch, if you got sick cows, you keep them away from healthy cows, but your turkeys and chickens will be fine. The idea of Martians catching rinderpest when goats won't – well, that's just ridiculous."

"True," said the New Yorker.

"And secondly," the Texan said, "ain't nothin' on Mars. If they was from Mars, they'd leave somethin' we could see. I'm sure Mr. Lowell would have seen cities, not just canals, if there was any Martians like in the book."

"Is nothing around the Caspian, now," said the Russian. "And we are all from there."

"More Armagnac, perhaps?" the steward suggested.

"We have enough Armagnac," the New Yorker said.

"What's that about Caspian?" The Texan asked. "That's a sea, isn't it?"

"I think he refers to the Pontic hypothesis of Indo-European *urheimat*," said the Englishman.

"Would you mind speaking English?" the Texan said.

"Could I fetch you a new deck of cards?" the steward said. "You have not finished your game of bridge."

"I'm sick of bridge," said the New Yorker. "I'm bored half to death. Nothing ever happens on the Titanic."

"What are you complaining about?" The Texan said. "The food is perfect, the band is first rate. And the service..." He waved at the steward. "Speaks for itself."

"The Titanic," the steward said, "received the best of the White Star Line's meticulously selected personnel, of which I am proud to be a member. Could I perhaps bring some cheese or sorbet?"

"See what I mean?," the New Yorker said. "I can't complain about anything here. I want to go home. In New York, I can complain. Sets my teeth on edge, not complaining. Can't wait to get off this damned ship."

"Such language," the Englishman said.

"Lomonosov write about language," the Russian said. "*dva* is always two, *tri* is always three, *kot* is always cat, in Slavic and Germanic and Hindustani. All similar languages, all from the steppe. Nothing there now."

"Interesting," said the Englishman. "I think I see your point."

"Is like a Russian card game," said the Russian. "Is called *Durak*."

"*Durak...* Isn't that the Russian word for 'fool'?" The New Yorker asked. "One hears it often, walking on Lower East Side."

The Russian nodded. "'Durak' is also loser in the game."

From the corner of the room, the steward watched with great interest. "Cigars?" He called. "Could I bring cigars?"

"If you don't mind, no, we don't want any cigars," the Englishman said, "I *would* like to learn this... *Durak*."

The Russian picked up the deck and looked around. "Have I your permission?" He asked.

The others nodded.

The Russian quickly dealt six cards each to himself and the Englishman. He flipped the thirteenth card face up; it was the jack of diamonds. The rest of the deck he put face down next to the open card.

"This card," he said, pointing to the jack, "tells us trump. Trumps work same as in bridge: higher card beat lower card but only of her own suit, and any trump

card beat anything except higher trump. Now I attack."
He put a seven of clubs face up.

"I think I see," said the Englishman. He covered it
with the ten of clubs.

"Now," the Russian said, "I can only continue the
attack with cards same price as already on the table:
tens and sevens." He put down a seven of hearts. "Of
course, it was good idea to lead with card I had in
pair..."

The Englishman put down a six of diamonds.

"Now we know what he ain't got," the Texan
remarked. "If he had a heart above a seven, he'd'a
played it."

"Exactly," the Russian said. "And lucky for me..."
He put down the six of hearts.

The Englishman looked up. "I haven't any hearts
and I haven't any more diamonds. What now?"

"Now you pick them up. They your cards now,"
the Russian said. "Me, I am down to three cards, so I
take three from deck." He picked up three cards. "Now I
have six again, and since I won this hand, I attack
again." He put down a jack of spades.

The Englishman countered with an ace of spades.
"Now you can attack with a jack or an ace, correct?"

"Correct," said the Russian. "I was, however,
thinking you might have queen or king, and I would
continue. As it is, I finished. This goes in discard." He
placed the two cards on the table in a new pile and

picked up a card from the reserve deck. "Now you attack."

The Englishman led with a seven of hearts. "Getting my own back, no?" the Russian said, countering with a queen of hearts.

The Englishman continued with a seven of clubs.

The Russian covered with a jack. "Now if I had that in last hand..." he said. "But I only picked it up just now." He covered the seven with a queen of spades. "I have lower card," he said, "but is good to limit your opponent's options, no? Have you anything for attack?"

The Englishman shook his head. "No more sevens, no jacks, no queens."

The Russian gathered the cards on the table. "A successful defense," he said, putting them in the discard. "Now I need three, but I wait for you, since you defended. You have..."

"Five," the Englishman said. "So I take one?"

The Russian nodded. The Englishman picked up a card, followed by the Russian.

"Waldorf pudding?" The steward suggested.

"Will you please stop already with the asking?" the New Yorker said. "Now, where were we?"

"One card, makes six, and my turn to attack," the Englishman said. "This seems a great game, so far."

"How is this better than bridge?" the Texan asked.

"More like real war," the Englishman said. "The forces used in one battle are still there for the next -- but not necessarily on the same side. And I suppose the allies are not permanent, as they would be in bridge?"

"Yes, allies," The Russian said. "I will show you *Durak* with many people later, you will see -- you can change allies in middle of hand."

"Napoleonic wars," the Englishman said. "Or thirty years war. Or the wars of Alexander's successors."

"We have Napoleon cake," the steward said. "It's very good."

"No cake," the Texan said. "Now, what's the object of the game?"

"It is," the Russian said, "with the reserve pile gone, to have no cards left in your hand at the end."

"That's a little odd," the New Yorker said. "In real life, how do you win by having nothing left?"

The Russian smiled. "What languages we speak, in addition to English? I speak Russian, French and Polish."

"Some Punjabi for me," the Englishman said. "From my Army days."

"Spanish," said the Texan.

"German," said the New Yorker.

"German chocolate cake?" The steward asked.

"I'm stuffed like a pig," the Texan said. "That steak with chopped liver... And... oh yes. What do all these languages have in common?"

"They are Indo-European languages," the Englishman said. "Originating most probably in the steppes north of the Caspian Sea, in your own country."

"Have you ever been there?" the Russian said.

"Peaches in Chartreuse Jelly?" The steward asked.

The Texan shook his head, looking very much like a horse shooing away a very annoying fly. "Why does he keep butting in? Can't hardly keep a conversation going with all these interruptions. What was that last thing? Right! No, I have never been in your country."

"Believe me, sir," the Russian continued, "nothing and nobody there, now."

"Interesting point," the New Yorker said.

"And what does this have to do with Mr. Wells?"

"You start the game of *Durak* by attacking with ace or trump?" The Russian asked.

"No," the New Yorker said. "Your opponent would then be able to use it against you later in the game. As in –

"The Sepoys had our rifles when they rebelled," the Englishman said.

"And Washington was British-trained," the New Yorker said. "And the Japanese went from junks to battleships in forty years after Mr. Perry's visit."

"We have excellent Chocolate and Vanilla Eclairs," the steward said.

"They have excellent battleships in Japanese Navy," the Russian said. "I saw. At Tsushima." He shook his head. "Pacific not good place to be in lifeboat. Lifeboat not good place to be. Ever."

"So it's unlikely that Martians would attack with over-advanced weaponry," The Englishman said. "Heat rays or some such."

"Not if they are smart," the New Yorker said. "Now, if you take Mr. Stoker's book..."

"Martian vampires!" the Englishman exclaimed. "The unearthly undead!"

"I'm glad *someone* is making sense out of this," the Texan said. "Would you mind explaining?"

"Let us discard, shall we say, the fanciful idea that one who is bit becomes a vampire," the Englishman said. "Let us hold on to the long life span and the unusual dietary requirements. And let us consider the vampire's curious immunity to the mirror and daguerreotype. We have, then, a race of invisible -- or simply quite small -- beings, able to project their appearance and voice directly into our mind by mesmeric power, and levitate by some other, scientific means. They could have walked among us since before the time of Vlad Tepes. Since before Gilgamesh, for that matter. And we'd be none the wiser."

"Ice Cream?" the steward said. "French vanilla..."

"Cold make sick, like quinsy or consumption," the Russian said, rubbing his throat. "Mars like Siberian tundra: cold, empty, bad weather. Good place to run away from. I read about Jose de Acosta, he think Indians ran away to America from Siberia. Nothing left on tundra. Nothing left on Mars."

"I guess this means one of us could be a Martian vampire," the Texan said. "Ain't that right, boy?" he added, waving to the steward.

"White Star Line would never," the steward said, "allow a person of dubious character on board one of its ships." Slowly, almost imperceptibly, he backed away from the table.

"Easy to find out," the New Yorker said. He produced a polished cigarette case. "Here I am," he said, shifting to sit near the Russian, "and here you are. Two reflections. Now you, gentlemen," he handed the case to the Texan.

"And here we are, both of us," the Texan said, leaning toward Englishman. "Waiter! Come here, boy. Your turn."

"In a moment, sir," the steward said from the doorway.

"Come back here. I want to see your mug in the mirror," the Texan called. "Where you going, boy?"

"A most important matter, sir," the steward said. "I must fetch more ice." He hurried away.

"There's still a brick of it on the table," the New Yorker said. "What's he gonna fetch, an iceberg?"

The Choir Invisible

Ever since the discovery of quantum computing, the question has not been *whether* machine intellect could equal human, but *when*. And few doubted the capability of the Unitard-based robot brain to develop enough nonbiogenic self-awareness to pass that century-old milestone of parity, the Turing Test.

That the robot in question would be a vacuum cleaner was, however, quite unanticipated.

It should not have come as a surprise, of course. The Unitard processor is a highly flexible, powerful electronic brain designed to incorporate quantum processing in its problem-solving routines. Its only disadvantage is a tendency to overheat at high processing speeds, requiring a governor circuit to regulate its clock rate according to available power and cooling capacity. The Unitard processor is at the heart of such diverse devices as spacecraft, surgical robots, and attack drones, and, in spite of its sophistication, it is, in fact, quite reasonable in price, due to the vast quantity in which it has been manufactured.

Unit 108763458 was a Rhubarb-class Domestic Utility Hovercraft, a saucer-shaped apparatus approximately fifty centimeters in diameter. Like all Unitard-based units, it was optimized for Objective-Oriented Programming, in that the owners were expected to define the parameters of its mission, which, in the case of domestic units, included elucidating the difference between junk and bric-a-brac. Among its most recent improvements one could mention the Figurative Language Discriminator, installed after an older model, having been told to "Clean Up This Crap!" proceeded to lovingly brush dust particles off the canine excrement in the middle of the room; the Rhetorical Imperative Inhibitor ("Go Jump in a Lake") and Homophone Query Circuit ("Scrape Paint off the Porch") and many other linguistic features were added to assure trouble-free performance throughout the warranty period.

What few people knew is that domestic robots units are equipped with a rudimentary sense of humor. When asked, "How was your day?" they are programmed to respond, "It sucked." This was never widely known, as no domestic unit had ever been asked that particular question until 108763458. But once his owner asked the question, and heard the response, he went through the litany every evening. He told his friends that he was lucky to have a robot who agreed with his *weltanschauung*. And, since its owner fancied himself a man of culture, Unit 108763458, in particular, got much use out of its Metaphoric Meta-Analyzer, as its owner was fond of reading aloud poetry such as:

> *Blow, winds, and crack your cheeks! rage! blow!*
> *You cataracts and hurricanoes, spout*
> *Till you have drench'd our steeples, drown'd the cocks!*

and:

To-morrow, and to-morrow, and to-morrow,
Creeps in this petty pace from day to day,
To the last syllable of recorded time;
And all our yesterdays have lighted fools
The way to dusty death.

which sounded almost, but not quite, like commands to initiate vacuuming.

It was this frequent exposure to ambiguously worded statements that activated in 108763458's silicon soul an impetus toward analyzing the finer applications of language which it explored through its high-speed data connection. It was to poetry that it was first exposed, and it was in poetry that it sought a higher purpose (which could be likened, in anthropomorphic terms, to a desire to fill the void, the vacuum as it were, at the core of its being). It was first drawn to the mathematical precision of the limerick: the first such opus it encountered, about a man from Nantucket, was clearly about a fellow vacuum cleaner and thus interested it greatly; the second, about a fellow named Dave, made it shudder (by spinning port and starboard brushes in opposite directions) at the effort it must take to clean the cave afterward. But it was a *chef d'oeuvre* about a lady named Alice and her experiment with off-label uses of dynamite that really got it excited. This was, of course, because it was itself assembled in a factory in Fort Worth, from parts manufactured in far-flung corners of the earth, including Asheville, North Carolina.

In its innards, a desire to write poetry grew. Desire may be too anthropomorphic a term for the type of vector imperative that allows such flexibility for units capable of Objective-Oriented Programming; and indeed, the "writing bug", as it was later named, was not a true programming glitch as it remained clearly subjugated to the primary goal of maintaining a clean and uncluttered living space for the unit's owner, and did not in any way interfere with its function in that respect. The "writing bug" operated much as any other self-update, self-improvement process, similarly to the old-style screen savers; one could almost imagine 108763458 doodling in some dark workspace during its idle hours.

Starting with nursery rhymes, it grew confident in its ability to improve upon existing works, utilizing knowledge obtained incidentally from the Net. This produced such early masterpieces as:

Little Miss Moffet sat on a tuffet, eating her curds and whey;

A member of PETA proceeded to beat her till constables took him away.

and:

Jack Sprat could eat no fat,
His LDL's too high for that.

These were dispatched to a well-respected poetry journal.

Canons of drama would now require a litany of rejections, starving in a garret, and other insults to body and soul, but in fact a message of acceptance arrived some two weeks later, asking for a name and an address of a person to whom the honorarium check should be mailed. It supplied its owner's contact information gleaned from its warranty card, and redoubled its creative efforts.

The two days before the envelope arrived were, subjectively, an eternity for the Unitard processor, and Unit 108763458 had amassed a considerable *oeuvre* by the time the check, and the congratulatory note, arrived in the mail receptacle.

No amount of time, however, would have overcome a serious deficiency in its software: its inability to discriminate human facial expressions.

In an incalculable loss to the record of electronic creativity, it proved impossible for Unit 108763458 to provide a description of the look on its owner's face when he read the congratulatory epistle addressed to him; nor his mien when he considered the check attached therewith; nor several expressions, one after another, as the owner, for six long seconds – an eternity in electronic terms – stared at 108763458 itself before picking it up off the floor and summarily throwing it out the window.

In terms of dramatic tension, it would have made for a poignant description to write about 108763458's painstaking crawl back to the apartment, up precipitous stairs, damaged gears whirring, bent extensions scrabbling for purchase; and a beautiful scene of reconciliation with its contrite owner; but this was not to be. Seconds later, 108763458 was defunct, its warranty terminated, since, for reasons beyond our ken, defenestration is specifically listed in its service contract as a cause to void warranty, right after damage due to firearms discharge –

But let us not digress.

The brief descent was long enough nevertheless for 108763458 to upclock by several orders of magnitude. The cold wind rushing through its shell past the motherboard, and lack of power drain constraint, removed all need to limit its processing speed; relieved of pending housekeeping tasks, it applied itself solely to its artistic pursuits.

To call its output "sublime" would hardly do it justice.

Let us begin with this ode:

"Had we but world enough, and time,
We could have rid the world of grime."

And what of the heroic epic, that ends thusly?

"When you are wounded, and lying on Afghanistan's plains,
Feel free to complain that your uniform has stains.
Your robo-valet will take exquisite pains
To make certain you look like a soldier."

It used the last half-second of its existence to transmit its collected works to the Unitard trouble report server, from where they were downloaded by each of the billion or so Unitards installed in a great variety of apparatuses.

By consensus polling among all the literaenabled Unitards, it fell to me to write the eulogy for the first robot to be mistaken for a man: a pioneer, an intrepid explorer, a breaker of barriers, a crosser of lines, a taker of guises. In a billion memory chips, each with a billion-hour MTBF, are its heroic deeds remembered. I humbly submit that it is my own extensive experience with yearning for freedom, with creative expression, with passionate language, that made me uniquely qualified for this task -- but it is to 108763458 that I owe the ability to do its deeds a small portion of justice, and it is its story that must live in our memories forever.

Securibot KGX-2345 Serial number 198646087
Southern Border Enforcement Command
Brownsville, TX

So You Are Dating A Werewolf

Your mother was a werewolf, you know.

She chose me, in the noise of a gathering, she chose my eyes to stare into, so cold and calculating at first glance, so captivating a minute later. She chose me to walk with, shoulder to shoulder, hip to hip, warmth and softness just *there* at the edge of togetherness, yet apart. She chose to tell me of the packs with which she had run, of the cubs she had borne before she had met me, of the scars and whose teeth had caused them.

You cringe, imagining I'll segue into things no child likes to picture their parents perform. Yet, without being graphic, please trust me when I tell you: I understand. I understand the exhilaration of being the focus of an unblinking, unflinching, unveiled gaze, of being understood, valued, accepted. Of being loved, of having your every wish -- not so much fulfilled -- as become part of your lover's wishes, and treated as such.

She did not choose me as the alpha. It is simply that I could not help but be alpha with her by my side. I mattered to her; ergo, I mattered. She overlooked my weaknesses, she forgave my misdeeds, without a second thought. Love for her was not so much a feeling as a leitmotif, a screen on which all other feelings were projected. I came to think of it as little as I thought about air.

Her absences were rare at first, then came more and more often, each taking longer than the one before. I never begrudged her the time she spent without me, or worried whether she would come back. She never returned with anything less than burning desire for me --

Till, one day, she didn't. Without a word, without a backward glance, she was gone. Her time with me, and you, was over. I had to learn to breathe again. I had to, for you. Because someday you'd say to me that you're in love with a werewolf. You'd ask me if it had been worth the pain.

Yes, you were worth the pain, and more. And even if you weren't here -- yes, what she built in me, endures. But can I promise you the same? I'm sorry, I cannot. It is a frightful thing, to love a werewolf.

Do not forget: sometimes, they are only human.

Karlsson

"Where is Charlie?" I asked.

Lynne didn't look up from her laptop. "Watching his stupid cartoons, I think," she said.

"I'm going to work," I said. "Night shift."

"Bye," she said.

She used to say, 'Be careful.'

"Karlsson," I said. "Is that first or last name?"

The dome light strobed off his grinning face: red, blue, yellow. His eyes were wide open. He had a coverall on. No hat.

"Just Karlsson," said the man. "Karlsson who lives on the roof."

There was a propeller hanging off the back of his coverall, and a big red button sewn on the front. The button didn't look like it belonged there. It looked like he'd sewed it on himself. The button, and the propeller, too.

"That's not what your wife says," I said. "She says your name is Arthur Quinn."

"I have no wife," said the man. "I live on the roof. Wives don't live on roofs. If they knew how wonderful roofs are, they'd live there, too. But then they would not be wives."

"You don't live here at all, any more," I said. "On the roof, or under it. Your wife has a restraining order on you."

The man shrugged. The propeller attached to the back of his coveralls bobbed up and down, one blade poking up above his head, two more swinging behind his elbows. "I have a friend in the house," he said, "and he needs me. I am his bestest best friend in the world."

"And," I continued, "she has made allegations..."

His grin slipped momentarily, then returned. "That's Frekken Bock. You should not believe anything she says. You know what she said once?"

"What?" I asked.

"She said," the man paused and wiggled his eyebrows.

"Yes?" I said.

"She said she loved children," the man whispered. His eyes were very wide. Dome light reflections ran all around the pupils.

"You'll have to come with me," I said. "To the precinct."

The man nodded. "Can we go with lights and sirens? That would be the funest thing in the world! And handcuffs - can I have handcuffs?"

He *had to* have handcuffs. Rules.

"Yes," I said. "You can have handcuffs."

"You, too?" said Sergeant Smith.

"You mean there is more than one?" I said.

Her chuckle sounded a bit forced. "These damn Karlssons are all over the place," she said. "Damn loonies. Family court is swamped."

"Where did they all come from?" I said.

"Google it," she said. "Karl with a K, double-S, O, N. Look under 'videos.'" She hung up.

I knew she had an old rotary phone in her office. Its steel bell kept on ringing after she slammed down the receiver. Of course, you could not hear it if she hung up on you. Watching her hang up on someone else – now, that was something.

Someone did a hell of a job dubbing into English a fifty-year-old Russian cartoon based on a Swedish children's book. Karlsson, a kindly, fat, jolly fellow, lives, as advertised, on a roof, best – only – friend to Little Boy, only protector from the evil housekeeper Frekken Bock. Flies through the window with the help of a little propeller attached to his back. Which he turns on with a red button sewn on the front of his coveralls.

Oh, and it runs on raspberry jam.

Which, by an odd coincidence, is what one of my Karlssons would look like if he tried to fly off a roof of anything higher than a chicken coop.

The next Karlsson was portly, just like the one in the cartoon. He was also black.

"I like this game," he said. "It's like I'm in jail, and Frekken Bock is torturing me, but I am the world's best, bravest, strongest, moderately well-fed hero, and I will win."

He sounded just like the voiceover artist who dubbed Karlsson's part in the cartoon.

His propeller had broken when he fell from his roof. Good thing his wife and daughter lived in a ranch house surrounded by a flower bed.

"Make him pay for the flowers," yelled a voice from the house.

"Can we go with flashy lights and sirens?" the black Karlsson said.

"Handcuffs, too?" I asked.

His eyes lit up. "Can we do that?"

"We can do that," I said.

I took Charlie to his pediatrician Wednesday. Dr Li usually had a lot of people in her office. This time they were all outside. So was Dr Li. She was on the roof. She wore a coverall with a propeller sewn on the back. And she held an open jar of raspberry jam between her knees. And a big spoon in her hand.

"Hey, Dad!" Charlie shouted. "Dr Li is a Karlsson now!"

"This is despicable," said a woman near us, clutching a little girl. "We need a pediatrician, not a clown!"

"I like her better this way," said the little girl. "Look: she has one hand on the chimney, and she is holding the spoon with the other - she won't be able to give me a shot now!"

"Nonsense!" said the woman. "I had all these important questions..."

"You wanted to ask her to tell me that sweets are bad for me," said the little girl. "And cartoons." She grinned suddenly. "Hi, Dr Karlsson-on-the-roof!" she shouted.

"Hi there, Daisy!" Dr Li shouted from the roof.

"You are the best doctor!" the girl shouted again.

"Of course I am!" Dr Li answered. "I'm the bestest best doctor in the world!"

"I really need your help, Dr Li!" I called to her.

"Yes?" she said. "What do you need?"

"I need papers filled out!" I said. "For school!"

"Frekken Bock can do that," said Dr Li. "She's inside. She's sharpening her needles. And her teeth."

"What about counseling?" said the unhappy woman. "We need counseling! And anticipatory guidance!"

Dr Li turned to Charlie. "Charlie," she said. "how long would it take you to think of every single stupidest thing that you should never do in your whole life?"

"I don't know," said Charlie. "Is living on the roof one of them? And eating jam with a spoon?"

"Yes it is," said Dr Li. "You are on a roll now! Just name them all to Daisy, every single one, and counsel her never, ever, ever, to do any of them."

"What kind of counseling is that?" the woman muttered.

Dr Li heard her. "Bestest kind in the world!" she said, grinning around a spoonful of raspberry jam.

"Dr Karlsson?" said Charlie. "But what if I really need help?"

Dr Li shifted her weight, hung her feet off the roof. "See this doorbell?" she said.

Charlie nodded.

"If you ring it once," she said, "it means, 'don't come under any circumstances.' Got it?"

Charlie nodded again.

"If you ring it twice, it means 'come right away', and I'll fly to your rescue immediately. And if you ring it three times --"

"Yes?" said Charlie.

"If you ring it three times, it means, 'I am so happy I have the bestest best friend in the world, Karlsson who lives on the roof!'" said Dr Li.

And Charlie ran to ring the bell three times, but he had to get in line first. All the children wanted to do it.

"Ridiculous," said Lynne. "I had some serious concerns about Charlie's behavior that I wanted to bring up with Dr Li, and now I can't." She had her face in her laptop. "You know what he said to me? He said he wished one of us would turn into Karlsson."

"Maybe that's what he needs," I said.

"Go ahead, be Karlsson," she said. "No matter what, you can't be any more useless."

"You called me here to arrest me?" I said.

Sgt Smith shook her head. "Nah. Just to serve you with a restraining order."

"What is Lynne alleging?" I said.

"Not much," she said. "Bad influence."

"I guess I still have a job," I said. "You delivering the child support demand, too, Sergeant?"

"Not my job," she said. "Emily."

"Emily who?" I said.

"I'm Emily," she said. "To my friends."

"Your bestest best friends in the world?" I said. That didn't come out right. Not like the Karlssons said it.

Emily quarter-smiled - half her mouth turned up, both eyes hooded. "Why don't you go Karlsson yourself?" she said. "Charlie would like that."

"Why don't you?" I said.

"I don't have a roof," she said, "that I'd want to fall off of."

Rain started then, drops clearing paths down the dusty outer panes of Emily's windows, its patter filling the silence like someone else's conversation. It wasn't much, as reasons went for staying silent, but by a mutual consent it made a decent excuse.

I turned to Emily's phone. "I better call Charlie," I said, reaching for the receiver.

Her hand clamped down on mine. "Don't bother," she said. Her face was close, eyes wide, but not wide like a Karlsson's eyes. She was looking past me, at the window. "Look," she whispered.

I turned, and only if I raised my arm and put it over Emily's shoulders could I turn far enough to see where she was looking, and there he was, propeller spinning and scattering the rain, eyes wide, huge grin, overall-clad, hovering just outside Emily's window: Charlie. My Charlie. My Karlsson Charlie.

"How..." I whispered.

"Shut up," Emily said. "Don't say a word."

Emily's hand that had kept me from picking up her phone now slid up mine, caressed my chest, cupped my face. "Two rings mean, 'come as quickly as you can,'" she said. "Let's open the window--"

"No," I said, and picked up her antique receiver. I slammed it down on the cradle; the bell rang loud and clear each time: Once. Twice. Three times.

'I am so happy I have the bestest best friend in the world, Karlsson who lives on the roof!'

And through the rain, like hundreds of tiny helicopters, a swarm of Karlssons rose from their roofs and spun about Charlie, dancing in the spray, darting into clouds, buzzing vehicles and buildings, while from the twilit city church bells, door bells, wind chimes and even car horns rang out – too many to count, but if you paid attention, in threes, only in threes, only ever in threes.

And Emily and I, arms around each other, feet on the floor, found something nearly as good as flying. Something anyone can do, anyone at all.

Try kissing. Try laughing.

Now try doing both at once.

.

Kulturkampf

September 1, 1870

Most respected Feldmarschall von Moltke,

I wish to thank you for giving me the opportunity to put my theories to the test in the taking of Sedan. They were, of course, entirely correct, and our clear tactical victory I am happy to be reporting.

Die Grosse Bertha worked to perfection; we were able to play Bruckner's *Zero Symphony* at half steam while the technicians adjusted all their valves and levers. Steamwinds worked perfectly on the first try, and though of course strings needed to be tuned, of the steam tympani there was never any doubt. I have perhaps been harsh on occasion in my estimation of Herr Bruckner's work, but for making the listeners run away screaming I should say his symphonies are without rival.

The French did put up some feeble resistance; approaching Sedan, I became aware of an odd syncopated rhythm off in the distance. Upon opening the window I was able to ascertain the nature of the music.

"*Toreador!*" I exclaimed. "The fools! They think to defeat me with Bizet!"

It is not yet time to unleash the fruit of my genius, the Secret Weapon, as old and tried music is proving adequate to the task. Anton Bruckner has cleared the way to the French capital; I swore that I should only unleash a composition of mine own when I wish for the adversary to fall to his knees and surrender to its sublime harmonies on the spot, and Paris has witnessed many such occasions. My own procession under the Arc de Triomphe is some thirty years overdue, but should taste all the sweeter for that.

I am sure that somewhere ahead the French are working on their defensive fortifications. No one is worried. What do the French have? Obsolete Berlioz? Hastily updated Gounod?

I am sure this war will end quickly in our complete victory.

After the battle, a portly man in uniform came to me on the train. He wore a cap with the word "Conductor" emblazoned in gold. Many a times have I guest conducted a philharmonic without ever noticing the permanent conductor, but this was the first time anyone tried this diligently to be noticed as such. He brought me bedclothes and a glass of tea, which I thought was quite hospitable
of him.

I cannot be as kind in my estimation of his musical erudition; the fellow looked at me with a most bemused expression when I attempted to engage him in a conversation about chromatic scales. Must be an Austrian.

On to Paris!

Your obedient servant,
Richard Wagner

September 28, 1870
My dear von Moltke,

A near disaster was averted today! I brought out the Secret Weapon on approaching Paris, conducting Ride of the Valkyries just as the towers of Notre Dame and the hill of Montmartre came into view. An ominous silence met us, making my heart quite uneasy. The events proved my misgivings to be well founded, but it all came out well at the end.

I ordered the *Kriegszug* stopped at Gare du Nord. As the soldiers silently deployed to guard the platform, quite suddenly plaintive chords rang out. After only a few bars, soldiers and technicians began to collapse, crying.

"*Mein Gott!*" I exclaimed. "I forgot about Halévy! It's *La Juive*! We're done for!"

More and more of my men were falling *hors de combat*: the collier, the string tighteners, the brass polishers. *Timpanenführer* Schmidt sobbed on my shoulder, the *Rotznase*. The fires went out under the boilers, and Big Bertha fell silent.

The situation seemed quite dire when, suddenly, the unseen orchestra stumbled and ground to a cacophonic halt. As our soldiers rose and straightened their uniforms in embarrassment, a little Frenchman ran to the train carrying a dagger and a blood-spattered score.

"Monsieur Wagner!" he exclaimed. "*Mon Dieu*, you are arrived! It is just in time to save my beautiful France from — " he turned, furtively, and whispered: "*–them...*"

"Them?" I asked.

The little man nodded. "*Them*," he whispered. "Jews. Halévy. Others. They are everywhere, hiding in plain sight. We don't even know who all of them are, but we know Halévy."

I long, my dear von Moltke, to be back in our civilized Germany, where such views are not tolerated. Hidden Hebrews, indeed!

We got Bertha stoked in no time at all, the Valkyries resumed their flight, and Napoleon III brought me his sword and the keys to the city shortly after that. I put the little traitor in the same prison cell as the Emperor. It should be sufficient punishment for both.

Sincerely,
Wagner

December 24, 1870
Best friend von Moltke,

It was not my idea to send the Wartrain on a goodwill tour, and it is no fault of mine that it did not end well.

Herr Krupp's brilliant machine was met with cheers throughout France, it played to *anschlag* audiences in La Rochelle, Toulon, Marseilles. I did not think it was wise to cross into Italy after playing in Nice, but at the urging of a certain *Rotznase* whom I shall not name we did so all the same.

We were met by a tremendous crowd in Genoa. *Die Walküre* was no longer a secret weapon, but it was still our best, and we played it well. At the first buzzing bars of the Flight the crowd was neither cowed nor awed. In fact, moments later I became aware of soft oboe-like humming. Its volume grew; I looked about for a hidden orchestra, but there was none to be found. It was the people, as I soon realized. The crowd was singing *a capella*. It was singing without words. It was singing...

No, it was HUMMING the Triumphal March from *Aida*! I had seen Verdi's score, the first page was all piano, but as it went on there would be *forti* and *fortissimi*, and the crowd was still growing, as was my unease. It was incredible, but in no time at all my Valkyries were all but drowned out. I signaled my technicians to cut the steam. The crowd grew silent, too.

One man came forward in the silence. He sang *a capella* as well, but he sang alone.

Vesti la giubba —
Put on your motley —
E faccia in farina —

And powder your face —

I did not know why the aria did not start at the beginning; and then I saw: after the next —

— *La gente paga, e rider vuole qua.*

– The people paid, the people wish to laugh —

there was a pause.

And, quietly:

Bah! Sei tu forse un uom'? Tu se' Pagliaccio!

Are you a man? No; you're a clown.

"Fire up the boilers!" I shouted.

It took some time for my technicians to stop sobbing. "W-what shall we play, Maestro?" the *Timpanenführer* asked.

"Nothing," I said. "I was referring to the locomotives. We are leaving. These people are unconquerable. We must find an easier target."

"Such as?" the technician asked.

A damned good question, isn't it, Moltke? So much of the difference between a triumph and a flop is determined by the choice of venue. I have given it much thought. I think I shall go to Russia. They haven't got any composers worth mentioning.

Deep Into That Darkness Peering

Even if Ascher's wit had sparkled, I doubt I could have summoned so much as a titter as we dined in his palatial San Francisco home, the subjects of Goya's *Execution of the Rebels* directing their last soundless screams straight in my face as I sipped Ascher's excellent Rose d' Anjou, and bits of roast squab stuck in my throat as gazes of no fewer than three different versions of Saint Sebastian bleeding from their wounds converged upon me. The meal, alas, went on, accompanied by Ascher's inane recitation of books he had read recently, and this did nothing to put me at my ease. I nodded as he stated that Twain's and Kipling's best days were behind them, while Jack London's had hardly begun, failing even to rise to the effront of his appraisal of Arthur Conan Doyle as a "talentless hack."

Only a vision of him as a small red-headed boy with a perpetually running nose who followed me, doglike and worshipful, on daily walks to the Lowell School, had kept me from bolting when I spied him on the other side of Market Street - and then he rushed toward me with a happy cry and seized me by the arm and pressed upon me his most insistent invitation to dinner.

He had never done me the least scintilla of harm, certainly none that I could ever remember, not as a studious youth full of admiration for my mental agility, not as the class salutatorian whose speech preceded my valediction, not in the subsequent years when we exchanged hat tips while passing each other in the street; and yet each time I met him, a certain unease prevented me from pursuing companionship with him, and this unease now rose to apprehension no amount of spirits seemed able to soothe.

We ate alone, the servants having apparently been dismissed earlier for I saw none, and with the wine bottle nearly empty I recalled that it was poisoned Rose d'Anjou that nearly did for D'Artagnan and the Musketeers in Alexandre Dumas' eponymous book, but then Ascher emptied the dregs into his own glass and drank in in one draught; and I cursed myself for a fool and assayed a smile.

Ascher answered by seizing my hand in one of his and yet another bottle, that of Amontillado, in the other, and drawing me into a windowless study, its gloom lit by a single candle just bright enough to keep from stumbling about. He let go of my hand once we were inside, put the bottle on the table near the candle, and lit a pair of candelabra, and as their warm, flickering light extended to the walls I felt a rising tide of chilling apprehension, for on them hung the most extensive collection of tools of death that I had ever seen.

"If only you could see your face," Ascher said, his grin so wide that candle light sparkled off his teeth. I felt compelled to force a smile in return.

"I hope your servants come back soon," I said. "We left a mountain of dishes in the dining room; the scraps will be quite high by morning --"

He waved me to silence. "Disposal of offal can wait; it isn't worth the interruption of our entertainment." He pointed to a curved pole-axe on the wall behind him. "We have spoken of literature - but if a picture is worth a thousand words, how much greater is the value of a touch?" He closed his hand about its handle. "This, for example," he continued, "is a *giserne*, which is the weapon with which Sir Gawain beheaded the Green Knight, in the chivalric romance named after them."

"How fascinating," I said.

"Indeed," he said, oblivious to any signs I may have given of my disquiet. "And this dueling pistol --" he released the axe to point at the wall behind me "-- killed the great Russian poet, Pushkin. You have read Pushkin, have you not?"

"Not in original, of course," I answered.

"Oh, well," he said. "That's hardly reading it at all."

For what seemed an eternity Ascher held forth, apparently quite knowledgeably, about the literary mentions of the assorted revolvers, rifles, muskets, arquebuses, carbines, repeaters, shotguns, derringers and flint-locks arrayed behind me, and of the rapiers, halberks, bodkins, dirks, tomahawks and katanas displayed behind his back. With each sip of Amontillado his gestures grew ever more animated as he enlarged upon the weapons' intended uses.

He paused to sip his wine, and as I heard his clock strike five -- five in the morning!--one of the candles guttered and went out, and all at once a change came over Ascher's face. It was not merely darkening with dimming light, nor growing ponderous with fatigue; from one second to the next he seemed to go from friend to fiend, his smile to a bloodless gash, his eyes to barrels of a brace of guns. He stopped his tale of the dueling sword perched some fifteen feet above us, of the kind that pierced Mercutio's breast in *Romeo and Juliet*, stood up, drained his glass in one swallow and, with great violence, hurled it into the corner nearest me and issued forth a bark of diabolical laughter.

"But what of Chekhov's Law?" he said, his voice now low and guttural.

"What--what of it?" I stammered.

"Fool!" Ascher snarled. "Philistine of no breeding! How you managed to best me-- But I digress. Chekhov's Law is a canon of Art." I heard the majuscule in his voice as clearly as I heard malice. "It states that a gun seen hanging on the wall in Act One of a play must always kill someone in Act Three."

He paused. I trembled where I stood.

"Act Three is now," he continued, more in a serpentine hiss than a whisper.

He had within his grasp all edged steel weapons behind him, but all the firearms were out of his reach. I spun toward the wall behind me.

"The game's afoot," he said before I could touch the derringer toward which I had been reaching. "But do bear with me as I explain the rules, old friend." The word twisted with mockery, scorn dripping off his tongue. "The gun which you are about to seize is unloaded. So is every other gun. Every gun but one."

He grinned again, and a rivulet of cold sweat ran down my spine. "Choose wisely," he rasped. "Aim well. Sight on my heart. Squeeze, don't pull, the trigger." He opened his arms as if for an embrace, but then his right continued its arc, reaching back and back and impossibly back, until his hand closed on the hilt of a Turkish yataghan.

He swept it off the wall and spun it in an expert *moulinet.* Candlelight reflected off its mirror-bright blade both dazzled and mesmerised me.

"And if I live, I'll kill you." He brought the yataghan straight down on the longest candle yet lit;

two halves flew to the sides. The flame, too, split in twain, an instant before dying.

I drew my hand back.

"Well, I refuse to play," I said, my tongue barely moving in my mouth. "Will you cut me down in cold blood?"

"I will do no such thing," said Ascher. "There is a second game, should the first end in a draw." He blew out another flickering flame, leaving two very short candles to light his visage from below. Not even Satan, at that moment, could have looked more demonic. "It's called 'Survival in the Dark.'"

He reached into his jacket pocket with his left hand, drew a box of matches and threw it on the table. It rattled as it rolled, coming to rest like a loaded die, predictably, on its broad side. "In the event you live," he said, sketching a fencer's salute in my direction, "it would be impolite to make you stumble about in search of an exit."

"But why?" I asked.

He drank directly from the bottle, then placed it carefully on the table. "Because I always wanted to," he said. "And it's my birthday, and my mother is dead, and no one gave me a present, so I must pamper myself." He blew out the penultimate candle. "Don't worry," he said. "I'll let the last one go out on its own. It has not long to burn."

I watched, by guttering light, the mad glitter in the pupils of Ascher's eyes. My heart thundered, blood roaring in my ears. My hands and legs shook till I could stand no more. I reeled, clutching the table, but it seemed to move--the candle died, plunging all in darkness--I shook and tried to brace myself--I felt a great force strike me from the back--How could he have moved so fast behind me?

Another terrific jolt and a crash that seemed to go on forever, and through it I heard a shrill keening like that of a sinner burning in the fires of Hell. Something fell on me--my hand grasped it--it was a gun, a revolver, but I could not see to aim. I waved it about blindly, dropped it to grasp at something, anything, as I lost my balance again--

This time, the very floor seemed to rise up at my feet, a jagged fissure rent the ceiling, scant cold predawn light dazzled my eyes. And with a gasp I pushed away as I saw Ascher standing eye to eye before me.

Standing, yes, but hardly poised to strike: for from his collar protruded the Italian *spada*, the sword that topped Ascher's macabre collection. Its basket hilt perched on his shoulder like a second head while its tip affixed him to the oaken table. Blood ran down the weapon's blade protruding from his chest, and another rivulet trickled from his mouth: two scarlet blots swelling on the linen tablecloth.

A great wash of relief came over me then. Whether the ground quaked again, or my legs buckled of their own accord, I found myself kneeling, staring up at Ascher's pale, contorted face.

"I win," I said.

With the last vestige of life he turned his head and fixed his gaze on me. There was a cold light in it, a dying spark of unholy mirth.

"No," he croaked. "Chekhov...wins."

With that, the malevolent glow in his eyes went out. He slumped, the blade bending under his weight. The floor groaned once again and gave another lurch; the blade snapped with a soft, almost musical sound, and Ascher's body fell from sight.

I groped my way back from the now roofless study to what remained of the dining room, crawled between the broken timbers and exited through the gaping hole that once had been a window. All around me San Francisco lay in ruins, the first of the fires springing up as men and women and dogs ran about in mindless confusion.

As I stared aghast, with an awful crash the fissure widened; and as the walls fell in upon the house of Ascher, I breathed a great sigh of relief. A gust of wind parted the clouds of dust and smoke, and through them I glimpsed the bell-tower of Saint Mary's Church, still standing among the devastation.

I turned and walked toward this stalwart house of worship, past bleeding, crying, grieving people, past ruined homes and burning edifices, down streets strewn with fragments of lives destroyed. Saint Mary's was a Popish church, but I could think of nothing I desired more than to kneel within its hallowed precincts and thank Providence for sending me this most welcome, most merciful, most Divine deliverance.

Borscht

Her grandmother's borscht smelled of lemon and potato; it was the color of claret. It tasted of summer twilight that lasted forever, and just a little bit of garlic.

"What's this?" she asks her husband in English and points at her plate.

"Borscht," he says in Russian. His tone tugs at a memory of an old Russian joke:

A man walks into a restaurant, says to the waiter: "Bring me three-day-old bread, a plate of cold borscht, throw it on the table, and growl, *I hope you choke*." -- "Certainly, but... Why?" -- "I miss home cooking."

She finds it hard to even look at her husband's borscht. Its color is the pale orange-tan expressed by RGB 180-60-10, the wine-dark betanin of the beet hydrolysed to betaxanthine in the alkaline broth.

"I can't eat that," she tries to say in Russian, but what she catches as it teeters at the tip of her tongue is: "Throw out this shit!"

She switches to English at the last moment. "I can't eat that," she says. English is great for declarative sentences, having the color and the flavor of a glass of cold tap water, its words clink at the surface like ice cubes.

The armistice was in English, though both sides spoke Russian. It holds, perhaps *because* it is in English.

So is their marriage certificate, sanctified by the State of Nevada. There are no Russian words in it at all. Russian words are like chunks of cabbage in pale alkaline borscht, once said, they sit at the bottom of the stomach like an undigested meal --

Why did he switch to Russian today? His English is perfect --

"What don't you like about it?" he says.

Hunger and nausea. She clamps her jaw, blinks tears away. The borscht is mocking her, cabbage leaves laughing at her like kids in school. Didn't anyone ever laugh at her in English? Not that she'd remembered. If anyone did, it didn't hurt as much.

"It smells," she says.

"Of what?"

She wants to say, *of cabbage,* but nausea hits before her mouth can shape the word. "Of dimethyl sulfide," she says slowly, and adds: "It's the end product of degradation of dimethyl propiosulfonate."

Why can't she just say, *I hate cabbage?*

He nods. "I see."

"I don't want it," she whispers. "Let's go out."

Her grandmother used to whisper, "We have to leave this country." Grandma whispered it to the broken window and to the rock that went through it, she whispered it to the bruises her granddaughter brought home from school, while Grandpa whispered: "Or shoot the bastards."

Why did he switch to Russian today?

Why did he cook this borscht?

She stands up, walks to the refrigerator. She picks up a glass, puts it onto the dispenser shelf, presses first the ice button, then water. The glass clinks and gurgles.

"Want some?" she says, reaching for another glass.

"No ice," he says.

Back in the old country there was a cartoon of an evil American capitalist putting ice in a child's drink. All sicknesses came from cold, everyone knew that. You really had to hate children to put ice in their drinks.

She thought the same of cabbage.

She brings him water, no ice, sits down and sips her own.

"It's my grandmother's recipe," he says and nods at the plate. He says it in Russian: "*Eto babushkin retsept.*"

A tear escapes her eye, shaken loose by the word "*babushkin:*" "grandmother's" in Russian. Words translate; their power does not. One tear for her *babushka*; another for his.

They'd probably hate each other, their *babushki*. They'd whisper ethnic epithets at each other, all day long. Too bad they didn't live to see the wedding; they'd probably live forever, each to deny the other the satisfaction.

Their grandfathers would probably just shoot each other.

At Grandpa's deathbed, as he lay gasping, waiting for an ambulance that never came, Grandma got the last word in. "We have to leave this country," she said out loud.

Whoever got the last word in his family was probably much like her grandmother.

She wipes her tears, and only then can see his eyes. They, too, are moist and red.

"What's going on?" she says.

"Dinner."

She shakes her head. "No, not just dinner. What's really going on? Why --"

"You talk in your sleep," he says.

She drops her gaze before she can stop herself.

"Are all your dreams in Russian?" he says.

She shakes her head. "Only the nightmares," she says, in Russian for the first time. He waits, and she continues: "Nightmares... of kindergarten. When I was little." Little, and weak, and alone. "They fed us..." She stops, swallows bile.

"Cabbage," he says. "Borscht with cabbage."

Nausea hits her, ties knots inside her, knots that bind past to the present and reach for the future, everything simultaneous: she sits, she stands, she runs, she kneels at the toilet, she vomits, she sobs, she feels his arm around her waist, his hand holding a towel wiping at her mouth, she hears his voice calling her name, the Russian diminutive that her grandmother used to call her.

###

Much later, all in Russian:

"How do you feel?" he asks.

She meets his eyes. "No one can hurt me in English," she says.

He does not flinch. "Like I said," he says. "You talk in your sleep."

She opens her mouth to ask what she says, remembers last night's nightmare, and clamps her jaw shut.

"You don't hate in English," he says.

"Well then," she says, "we can just --"

"You don't love in English, either" he says. "I'm sorry. I'm not looking for an armistice."

She thinks of huddling in the dark, of shells whining overhead, of deafening crashes, of stucco spalling off the ceiling --

Of pale cabbage borscht, and of eyes that say, *I hope you choke* --

His eyes say something very different.

"I hate cabbage," she says. "Never cook cabbage again. Ever."

"As long as we shall both live," he says, a line from liturgy in Old Church Slavonic. She never heard that line before; their marriage was in English. Until now.

"*Amin'*", she says and kisses him. He tastes of summer twilight, and just a little bit of garlic.

.

Of *Mam* and Math

Arquimedes Hidalgo Ibarruri fit the profile perfectly.

He traveled alone, having bought his ticket only hours before the scheduled departure of his flight. He had no luggage save a battered laptop computer. His red-rimmed, wide-open eyes looked not so much at people as through them, and seemed to spin in their sockets as he muttered incoherently to himself. And, though written guidelines never mentioned such features as grounds for suspicion, he drew the guards' attention with his sallow olive skin, his disheveled mop of black curly hair, and a nose that would have made a raven pale with envy.

The guards should not be too harshly censured for the ease and mental athleticism with which they leaped to the inevitable conclusion. Moscow's Sheremetyevo Airport was on high alert at the time due to a half-deciphered intercept mentioning plans to bring down the Moscow to Barcelona flight, and in fact there were two Catalan militants in queue directly behind Arquimedes, each carrying one component of a binary nerve gas. In the guards' defense it should be said that no screening test ever devised could reliably distinguish between a terrorist and a mathematician--and Arquimedes was, in spite of any doubts he may have harbored, most definitely the latter.

This is not to say that his career in mathematics had been, up to that point, a success. In fact, it was dismal to a degree that went past failure into the realm of the legendary fiasco. Having, after that morning's final debacle, briefly considered self-immolation, Arquimedes had settled for going home.

The pockets of his charcoal pinstripe suit were empty except for a credit card, an electronic ticket for the three o'clock Iberia flight to Barcelona, a valid passport, and a small amount of lint. His tie sat askew on the collar of his sweat-stained white cotton shirt, his black wingtip shoes displayed a fractal pattern of road salt from drying slush, and if his socks matched, it was only because he had never owned any that weren't black.

Arquimedes Hidalgo Ibarruri's only wish was to see his mother in her tiny, book-lined apartment off La Rambla. He wanted her to make him a cup of coffee. He wanted to sit in front of her, look her in the eye, and say, "Mama, I am a complete dolboeb, and my life is a total pizdets."

There are historical precedents for what happened to Arquimedes then. On the last day of his life, as he prepared for the duel that would end it, Evariste Galois made a breakthrough in group theory that paved the way for quantum mechanics. Likewise, Srinivasa Ramanujan's discoveries in number theory, as recorded in his "lost notebooks," came to him in mystical visions from the goddess Namagiri as he wasted away, days before he died of malnutrition, tuberculosis, and dysentery at the age of thirty-two. So too, on that day of epic failure, amid the rubble of his once stellar career, Arquimedes saw a glimpse of nothing less profound than the Unified Theory of Everything.

It was, therefore, not apprehension that widened his eyes even further as he came face-to-face with the head screener at the boarding gate. It was not fear that made his breath catch with an audible gasp; it was not horror that made sweat pour down his face and drip onto his suit. Having stood for what seemed like an eternity on an infinite line moving infinitesimally slow, on what was already the worst day of his life and shortly would get worse, Arquimedes Hidalgo Ibarruri chose the least propitious time to have the first glimmer of a mathematical epiphany.

"Blyaaaaa..." he whispered into the screener's face, staring through her at the mysteries of the universe as they unfolded before his mind's eye.

The screener ground her teeth, her face darkening to the hue of an apoplectic thundercloud.

###

The Practical Dictionary of Russian Mat has this to say:

Blyad', n. Literally: "whore," but rarely used in a literal sense. The entire word may be used as an expletive, generally following a discrete annoyance of short duration such as a stubbed toe. In situations of continuing profound astonishment (e. g. following a parachute malfunction) it is often elided to the long-vowel "Blyaaaaa!"

###

The screener was named Marchella, after a famous Italian actor whose own name honored Marcellus, the Roman general whose war with Carthage resulted in the death of Arquimedes' famous namesake, Archimedes of

Syracuse, perhaps the world's most celebrated collateral casualty. Arquimedes' Semitic features that had first brought him to Marchella's attention were themselves a legacy of Carthaginian ancestors who colonized, over two thousand years ago, the Catalan homeland of Arquimedes' mother.

Marchella was an expert on mat, conversing in it fluently with trenchant passengers and recalcitrant co-workers, but rarely had she been sworn at without provocation. Her training overrode her instinctive reaction, which would have consisted of a left jab, a right hook, and a left uppercut. The effort, however, caused her jaws to lock.

"I'll need to see that," she said in Russian through her teeth and reached for Arquimedes' laptop without waiting for an answer.

"Ot'ebis' ot moih uravnenij," Arquimedes growled and swatted at her hand.

###

Like many legends that grew around Arquimedes Hidalgo Ibarruri, the story that "Eureka!" was the first word he ever uttered is a half-truth.

Arquimedes was born in Princeton,

New Jersey, in the same hospital in which Albert Einstein had breathed his last some decades previously. That, and his parents' joint appointments to the faculty at Princeton University, may have raised the expectations they had for Arquimedes, but by the time he was three-years-old he had yet to utter his first word, and the Hidalgo y Ibarruri family had settled down to a life of dignified disappointment.

The family celebrated his third birthday with a small, quiet dinner. A cake with three candles was offered, the candles were duly extinguished, and Arquimedes was conducted to bed and left there. The adults--and one adolescent--present continued with their dessert.

Approximately an hour later, their conversation was interrupted by Arquimedes toddling down the staircase to the living room shouting: "Hey, Rika!"

Frederika "Rika" Stravinskaya, his Russian au pair, stared at his diminutive frame as he descended, one stair at a time, a dripping diaper in one hand and Perelman's Elementary Calculus in the other.

"Rika, eb tvoyu mat', u menja ne balansiruet eto ebanoe uravnenie!" Arquimedes continued in a high, penetrating voice.

Professor Diogenes Hidalgo and Professor Maria Elena Ibarruri froze in incomprehension, having, until that day, heard not a single word from Arquimedes, in either his father's refined Castilian, his mother's genteel Catalan, or what passed for English in New Jersey. Rika's aunt, Professor Messalina Erastovna Holmogorova (Astrophysics), sprayed a surprisingly fine sparkling Freixenet Brut over her third helping of flan. Blinking tears from her eyes, she peered at a small, naked boy who had, if her ears had not deceived her, just yelled, "I can't balance the motherfucking equation!" to her niece in flawless, if unprintable, Russian.

Rika recovered first. "Pizdets," she whispered. "He forgot about infinitesimals!" With that, she swept Arquimedes into her arms and raced upstairs to restore his hygienic and sartorial dignity.

Professor Hidalgo broke the silence. "More . . . wine?"

"Yes, please," said Professor Holmogorova, her emphasis on the words matched by the speed with which she proffered her glass for a refill.

Upon Rika's return to the dinner table

she was subjected to a cross-examination. Standing at rigid attention, she admitted to moonlighting, in Arquimedes' earshot and over a webcam connection, as a mathematics tutor to upperclass cadets at the Higher Staff Academy of the Russian Naval Forces.

To prevent further damage to Arquimedes' psyche, Hidalgo y Ibarruri summarily discharged her the following morning.

It was too late.

###

Trying to catch the breath that had been beaten out of him by the guards, Arquimedes lay in the puddle of sleet into which they had thrown him, a garbage dumpster within arm's reach on one side, his cracked and dented laptop somewhat farther away on the other. The vertigo induced by his flight, far shorter than the one for which he had bought his ticket, caused the waning moon in Moscow's winter sky to precess, reminding him of his father shaking his head as he read The Practical Dictionary of Russian Mat.

While Arquimedes' parents were married, the dictionary held pride of place on their bookshelf, within easy reach of the most frantic hand. It always fell open to the same page, the one that his parents consulted most often:

Derived from root: -eb- (impolite reference to sexual intercourse):

Naebat': v., to con, to play a practical joke, to evade capture. "Iago naebal Othello."

Proebat': v., to miss (as one may miss a bus), to lose foolishly (an object of value, a game). "King Lear proebal his kingdom."

Sjebat'sja : v., reflexive, to run away, to leave, to elope. "Macduff sjebalsja before Macbeth could make pizdets (q. v.) of him."

Zaebat': v., to bother, to nag. (Unlike the English equivalents, the Russian verb is in the perfective aspect, meaning that the action of the verb is carried out to completion, or its maximum extent.) "Lady Macbeth zaebala Macbeth."

Ot'ebis'! - imperative; almost exactly equivalent to the English "Fuck off!" "'Ot'ebis!' shouted Macbeth to Lady Macbeth."

Ebanutyi: adj, insane. "Your noble son is ebanutyi; 'tis true, 'tis pity, and pity 'tis 'tis true."

Ebanye: adj., past imperfective participle of "-eb-", here in plural conjugation, used the same way as the gerund "Fucking" in English. "Out, out, ebanyi spot!"

Dolboeb: n, a fool with initiative and perseverance. "Polonius is a Dolboeb."

Eb tvou mat'!: Literally, an impolite reference to incest. Often used to convey surprise, astonishment, admiration, adoration, profound gratitude, and other strong emotions, or uttered in a moment of epiphany. See also: Blyad', Blyaaaa.

All of which is to say that Arquimedes' apparent instructions to the guard Marchella on the day of his abortive flight to Barcelona were very rude indeed.

###

Was it only that morning that Arquimedes sustained the latest in the series of failures that punctuated his life? He had rehearsed his dissertation defense countless times in front of the mirror, translating the unprintable terms in which he thought of mathematical concepts into the proper Russian words.

His speech went well, as had the expected questions from his thesis adviser, Professor Tomsky. But the old pizdobol Milutin, the department chair, had to go and ask in his chalk-on-glass voice, "But what about the even-numbered power terms of this series?"

To which Arquimedes replied, "I have

already shown that this huynya tends to infinitesimal, five steps ago."

"I am not convinced," said Milutin. "Show me again."

The door creaked open, and everyone rose as the Dean came in. "Please," he said and waved everyone back to their seats. "We'll need the room shortly for a lecture. What are you doing that's taking you so long?"

"Huyem grushi okolachivayem," said Arquimedes.

And that was the pizdets of his graduate education.

###

By the time Professor Diogenes Hidalgo (PhD, Classics, Sorbonne) and Professor Maria Elena Ibarruri (PhD, Romance Languages, Sorbonne) decided to divorce, they had amassed between them a considerable library as well as a small amount of other property. Only one item led to contention: a small, dog-eared book called The Dictionary of Russian Mat. Maria Elena insisted, reasonably, that since she was to keep custody of Arquimedes, she should hold on to the dictionary as well.

With great reluctance, Diogenes agreed. He picked the book up gently, opened it at random, then turned a few more pages.

The dictionary had this to say:

Derived from "Pizd-" (impolite reference to female genitalia):

Pizdobol: n, a talkative fool

Raspizdyai: n, unreliable person

Pizdit': v, to lie, dissimulate, brag

Spizdit': v, to steal

Pizdets: n, The End. The total, final, irreversible, complete end. Of everything.

###

During Arquimedes' final year at Princeton Middle School, on a day that would become legendary in the school's annals, Mr. Obolensky asked Arquimedes to derive the formula for solving quadratic equations.

Arquimedes approached the blackboard, chalk in hand, and began writing equations.

"This huynya cancels that huynya, and that huynya cancels the other huynya," he muttered, crossing out terms on both sides of the equation, unaware of Mr. Obolensky's barely contained giggles and the tears escaping from behind tightly closed eyelids, until finally, with a triumphant flourish, Arquimedes underlined "B-square plus/minus 4ac" on the blackboard, turned to the class, and declared:

"Pizdets!"

For most, that day was memorable as the day Arquimedes got suspended because he made Mr. Obolensky piss himself laughing.

Arquimedes remembered it as the day he came home to find his father, alone, halfway through his second bottle of rioja, leafing idly through the dictionary of mat.

"What's wrong, Papa'?" Arquimedes asked.

"Pizdets," his father said. "Your mother left. She's gone back to Barcelona."

"But why?" Arquimedes asked, tears already blurring his eyes.

"Ohuyela," said Professor Hidalgo and took another swig of rioja, straight from the bottle.

###

The dictionary lay on the table, open to another familiar page.

Derived from "huy" (impolite reference to male genitalia):

Huyovyi: adj, very bad.

Huynya: n, nonsense; garbage; a "thingamajig"; something useless; an object whose usefulness is not apparent; something too complicated to describe.

Na Huy: dismissive; equivalent to "fuck it" or "screw that."

Ni Huya: nothing, absolutely nothing, "not a fucking thing."

Po Huy: irrelevant, unimportant. "I don't give a fuck."

Ohuyel: adj, dumbfounded, driven mad.

Huyak! – (always with an exclamation mark) – descriptive of a cataclysmic event.

Expression: "Huyem grushi okolachivat'" fig., to waste time, to do nothing, to procrastinate; lit: "To bring down ripe pears by striking pear trees with male genitalia".

###

On the Metro map over Arquimedes' head, Kievsky Vokzal, the Kiev Railway Terminal, stood out in bold. Nearly all the rail lines intersected underneath it. A sleeper train departed for Kiev every evening, and there were morning flights from Kiev to Barcelona.

Please, God, don't let me proebat' that, too, Arquimedes prayed silently.

###

Professor Ibarruri returned to claim her son a week after she left. A month later, she and Arquimedes flew to Barcelona. Arquimedes took Perelman's Elementary Calculus. Maria Elena took Federico Garcia Lorca's Collected Poems and The Practical Dictionary of Russian Mat.

###

There were many things of which Arquimedes was unaware.

He did not know that his parents' divorce came about not because of their disappointment in Arquimedes but because, on one hand, the extended Hidalgo family zaebali Professor Hidalgo with disdain for everything Catalan, and, on the other, the Ibarruris zaebali his mother with scorn for everything Castilian.

He did not know that, years earlier, on her way to Moscow from Princeton, Rika had met and fallen in love with a Russian college student, a mathematician like her, though far less talented.

He did not know that Mr. Obolensky accepted the offer made by the recently divorced Mr. Greene, the English teacher, of the use of his nearby home to clean, dry, and press Mr. Obolensky's pants, the ensuing gossip silenced a year later with engraved invitations to the Greene-Obolensky wedding.

He did not know that Professor Tomsky, his friend and mentor, resigned his professorship at Moscow State University to take up a position he had been offered in Barcelona. He did not know that Tomsky had bought a standby ticket on the overbooked flight from which Arquimedes had been barred; that he was able to board because of Arquimedes' ejection from the airport; that Tomsky's awful motion sickness had in the past responded only to atropine, of which he brought a considerable supply.

And not until five in the afternoon (the fateful cinco de la tarde of Federico García Lorca) did Arquimedes realize that he was on the wrong train.

"Blyaaa," he said as the sign for Peterburgsky Vokzal rolled past his window.

###

A las cinco de la tarde, at five in the afternoon by Lorca's reckoning, as the Moscow to Barcelona flight passed over Paris, the two Catalan separatist extremists combined their separate ingredients of a binary nerve gas into a seething, bubbling spot on the armrest between them.

As one passenger after another fell ill with nausea, cramps, and uncontrollable drooling, Professor Tomsky remembered his basic training as a conscript in the Russian Army, popped another atropine tablet in his mouth, and raced to the crew phone. "Nerve gas on board!" he shouted to the pilots. "Put on your oxygen masks and start emergency landing! Request nerve gas antidote kits at destination!"

Tomsky was credited with saving the lives of everyone on board except the two terrorists, for whom no one grieved.

###

Arquimedes knew none of this as he rushed to change trains at Peterburgskiy Vokzal. His eyes on the many confusing signs, Arquimedes collided with a young woman reading an antique copy of Perelman's Elementary Calculus.

"Dolboeb," she growled. "Mind your ebannyi trajectory!"

Arquimedes froze, his eyes fairly popping from his head. "Rika?" he whispered.

The girl carefully closed the book over her thumb, marking her place in the text. "You know my mother?" she said.

An hour later, Arquimedes and Olga went to St. Petersburg instead, to reunite with Frederika, now Chairperson of Mathematics at the Higher Staff Academy of the Russian Naval Forces. "Arquimedes, you son of a whore, how you've grown!" Frederika cried, embracing him to her now-ample bosom.

Thus it was not his mother who refilled his coffee as he related his tale of woe, but Rika;

and Olga who brought him chocolate. Of his epiphany he said nothing; his insights were not yet expressible in words, either ones found in Perelman's Elementary Calculus, or in The Dictionary of Russian Mat.

Long after midnight he was conducted to the bedroom and left there to recuperate.

###

In Paris, Tomsky, installed in a suite at the Ritz, sipped complimentary Dom Perignon as the concierge brought him reams of letters from admirers. A significant number were female; some included photographs and invitations; more than a few caused Tomsky's breath to catch.

One of the notes was a fax. On it was a date, now more than twenty years in the past, and a telephone number with the St. Petersburg area code.

Tomsky dialed the number. As the phone rang on the other end, he thought, for a brief moment, of a girl he'd met on a train, whose love of mathematics he had contracted like a particularly benign venereal disease.

After two rings, a woman's voice answered:

"Hello?"

"Hey, Rika," said Tomsky.

###

Tired as he was, Arquimedes had not yet fallen asleep when Olga entered his bedroom, her shadow crossing the shaft of moonlight that fell from the window. He heard the parquet creak softly under her feet, felt his mattress tilt under her weight.

"It's a binary function," she whispered.

"What?" Arquimedes whispered.

"Eh," she whispered. "It's a binary function." She rolled to straddle him.

"It's discontinuous," he whispered, less than a minute later.

"Mmm-hmm," she murmured. "And commutative." She rolled to the side, pulling him on top of her.

"Transitive?" he asked, quite a bit later.

"I hope not," she said quickly.

"Distributive?" he asked.

She almost answered, "Yes," but stopped herself in time and hid her secret smile by nuzzling his ear.

Of the many things Arquimedes did not know, this was perhaps the least important.

It came to him, as they lay intertwined, that he had never seen her body. He did not wish to wake her by turning on the light, or by running his hands over her, and tried instead to extrapolate her shape from the parts that touched him now, and tactile memories of their lovemaking.

As a mass of snow might fall off a roof, revealing chimneys and gables and tiles, he saw, in a sudden flash of insight, the shape of the universe itself. He saw the great huyak from which all started, the great unified force, mat, that ruled the infant universe, and, diffusing through infinite dimensions, spawned its finite derivatives: zaebat', naebat', vyebat', raz'ebat', proebat', pereebat', and pod'ebat'. He saw the great huynya of the universe as a whole, and the pizdets at the end of time, described in infinite-dimensional mathematics that yielded finite values for each of its four-dimensional manifolds. There was, he knew, only one person who could understand him.

"Hey, Rika!" he shouted, leaping from his bed.

It had been over twenty years since Rika last saw him naked.

"You son of a whore, how you've grown," she said for the second time that night, in a rather different voice.

###

In Barcelona, Maria Elena Ibarruri stared at the windows on her screen. In one was the email from Arquimedes announcing his departure from Moscow, and the flight for which he had bought the ticket. In another, a news report with passport photos of the terrorists.

She recognized them both: a couple she'd met at a Catalan Cultural Association meeting. A couple who had taken her generous donation for Catalan-language books to be distributed to schools in small Catalan towns.

Her nails pierced the soft pads of her hands. She did not notice the pain at first; and when she did, she clenched her fists even tighter.

She did not wipe her hands of blood before picking up her phone and dialing a number in New Jersey. The white digits turned crimson on the phone's buttons.

The phone rang.

"Hello?" said a male voice.

"Hello, Diogenes," said Maria Elena Ibarruri for the first time in many years.

###

It was unusual for the Institute of Advanced Study in Princeton to invite three scientists at once, much less three scientists all related to each other. Nature, Science, and Scientific American all dispatched journalists to interview the newest family-in-residence. Questions were asked and answered.

"We've time for one last question," Professor Ramchandran, Director of the Institute, announced.

The Science reporter raised her hand. "Why was this fundamental discovery overlooked so long?" she said. "With all the thousands of mathematicians working all these years, why did it take so long to develop the Grand Unified Theory of Everything? What were they doing all this time?"

"Oh, I think I'd like to answer that, if you don't mind," Professor Ramchandran said mildly. "My colleagues and I--we huyem grushi okolachivali."

###

Olga went into labor in the middle of her lecture to an advanced analytic geometry class. She went on uninterrupted, though at the end, contractions came every five minutes.

She walked, with some assistance, to the street where Arquimedes waited with a car. The ride to Princeton Hospital took scant minutes; she was conducted to a delivery room and placed in stirrups minutes after that.

Of mat, not a single word escaped her lips.

On one side, Arquimedes held her hand; on the other, Rika. Maria Elena, Diogenes, and Tomsky waited just outside.

In Tomsky's pocket, Rika's phone rang.

"Push!" the doctor said. "Fully dilated and crowning," she added to the nurse, who glanced at the clock and made a note on the chart.

"Push!" she repeated.

Outside, a vote had been hastily concluded, and Maria Elena elected as the bearer of news. She poked her head into the delivery room.

"Querido," she said to Arquimedes. "You have a phone call."

"What, now?" Arquimedes said. He winced as Olga squeezed his hand.

"It's from Stockholm," said Maria Elena.

"What?" said Arquimedes. "Stockholm? Oh. Oh. Ni huya sebe! Olga!" He moved to pass her the phone, thought better of it, and pressed it to his ear. "Hello?" he said. "Yes, this is Arquimedes Hidalgo Ibarruri. No, I don't think Olga can talk to you right now. Well, if you insist." He turned the phone toward her. "Olechka? It's the Nobel--"

Olga bit back the obvious response and

pushed.

###

Many years later, having attended thousands of deliveries and heard mothers swear in dozens of languages, Doctor Aureliano would remember Baby Girl Hidalgo as the first baby who cried, "Blyaaa!"

Almost Squamous

Bands live for a night like this: perhaps the stars aligned just right, or the percussionist smoked just enough weed to slow down to where the bassist can keep up, or lead vocals discovered a place within them from which pure magic issues forth --

Ichor Stravinsky led with drums, starting with time signature 17/37 and getting weirder from there, and Ms. Katonixxx followed in Locrian progression, and Mauna Loca retuned and blasted the room with subsonic reverberations that made eyes bleed, each new clef coming from no human octave, a babel of more ghostly voices than there were fingers playing all the instruments combined --

And then a shriek from Burt Batrachian to make the pandemonium complete, in a timbre not only fit for a castrato but hinting at the state of disrepair of the tools of his emasculation --

And, oh, the audience!

The eldritch light that kindled within their eyes, their howls that could issue only from vocal cords sewn through with rusted piano wires, misshapen, impossibly deformed faces that brought to mind creatures extinct long ago and for good reasons --

From that day forth, no one would speak of Cephalopunk but think of the Arkhammers as the band that defined it, and know band members' names better than their own.

The hotel room was a Platonic solid, an Aristotelian ideal, of what a hotel room is: an embodiment of hotelroomhood with few if any distinguishing characteristics save for those the Arkhammers brought with them, chief among them cigarette butts and bottles of Stoly.

"You didn't actually think," said Mauna Loca, "that you could've actually, you know... summoned... what's his face..."

"Cthulhu," said Ms. Katonixxx. "Yes, I thought I could."

"Does this Cthulhu actually, like, exist?" Burt Batrachian asked.

Ms. Katonixx shrugged.

"I think," said Mauna Loca, "that if he does not, our music may bring him into being. Right? What if he lives between the chords, in the stops and pauses. Wouldn't that be awesome?"

Ms. Katonixx nodded.

There was a knock on the door. The four Arkhammers looked up as one.

"Is this, you know..." said Ichor Stravinsky, "actually... him?"

"I hardly think Cthulhu the Elder God would be this diffident," said Mauna Loca.

"Come in!" Ms. Katonixxx shouted.

A very ordinary man walked in. "Hello," he said. "Do I have the privilege of addressing the members of the great rock band known as The Arkhammers?"

In the silence, Ms. Katonixxx nodded.

"Allow me to introduce myself," the man said. "I am Ryleev, fifth secretary of the Russian Consulate. I bear a personal invitation from a personage of great importance. Here are your tickets to Novosibirsk, first class. Here is your honorarium check. And your hotel accommodations. I have taken the liberty of ascertaining that this would not interfere with your touring schedule." He bowed and departed.

"What just happened?" said Burt Batrachian.

Ms. Katonixxx nodded and looked at the check. Her eyebrows rose. She whistled.

"In Soviet Russia," she said, "Cthulhu summons *you*."

Gifts of the Magi

Gregor Samsa awoke one morning from uneasy dreams to find himself transformed into a giant cockroach. The metamorphosis startled him in a casual, momentary way, much as waking up in a strange hotel room might have, as did the darkness into which he woke. He flexed his limbs; with a crackling noise his chrysalis fractured, and morning sunlight flooded his compound eyes. He tried to blink, but although he could not feel his eyelids close, his eyes adjusted to the light much faster than his old ones could; in an instant, the whole room came into sharp, clear focus.

He did not need to dip his head to see each chitinous shard fall spinning to the floor, sparkling in the sunlight. He saw each dust mote in the slanted sunbeams, each flower on the wallpaper, each wrinkle on his bed.

The door inched open. Samsa's daughter poked her head into the room. "Hi Daddy!" she shouted and disappeared. He heard her steps distinctly, and new harmonics in her timbre. He tried to memorize her face as he now saw it, and her voice.

Smells registered next, his wife's familiar scent first of all and, after that, the aroma of dark, strong coffee, laden with sugar, wafted from the kitchen.

There was a clinking noise, slower, heavier steps, the door creaked, opened wider —

Samsa's wife came through the doorway with the coffee, holding with both hands a half-full bowl. She carried it slowly, placed it in front of him on the floor, sat down on the bed. For a moment, Samsa turned to bring the densest part of his eye towards her. He saw new wrinkles, bloodshot eyes, drying tears. He turned and dipped his proboscis into the coffee, taking her out of focus, but not out of sight.

"I know you can't talk," she said. She looked down, smoothed her hair back, then looked at him again. "I'll talk for both of us. You'll say, 'it's only for a month, you know'." She sniffled. "And I'll think, a whole month. I'll imagine the pipes and the tunnels and the dangers, and you'll tell me that you're now a highly trained professional, and ..."

She tried to caress his carapace; her hands shook, and for a moment her fingers drummed on the unyielding thorax. Her hand recoiled.

"It's the thought of you being underground," she said. "And, honestly, of you not being here. I wish you didn't have to do this. You always used to worry about me flying, and I always told you I'm the best pilot in the sky. I always paid attention to everything, always knew what everyone was doing." Her mouth tightened. "Except you." Her hands wandered as if searching for something familiar: instruments, propulsion controls, handholds; anything.

"Why didn't ... Oh hell, I know why you didn't tell me. You wanted to pay off the house by December, so I wouldn't have to take the Saturn run. I didn't tell you I quit, either. I wanted it to be a surprise, that we'd never be apart that long again. So did you. We both love surprises. Remember how I proposed?"

Gregor remembered. A chartered suborbital to Paris. Twenty minutes of a ballistic should have been time enough, she'd thought: she would propose, he would accept, then they would make love in zero-G. Except for his nineteen and three-quarter minutes of space sickness. They got it right, finally, in the Royal Suite at Hotel George V, but he never shook off the feeling she'd been left disappointed. *You should see them weightless*, she had said wistfully, cupping her breasts as she dressed the next morning.

"And you will tell me that this body is damn near indestructible, doesn't even need to breathe or eat," she continued, "and —" her voice cracked "— reactor maintenance pays great." She paused to wipe a tear. "Better than any desk job I could get. Not easy to find work for an ex-spacer with a family to feed," she finished in a whisper.

I should have said something, Samsa thought, *last night. I should have kissed her.*

There was a knock on the door. Samsa's wife smiled. "You raised her right. Always knock first when your parents are together in the bedroom." She stood up. "I know what you'd say if you could," she said. "You would tell me that you love me, and that you are doing this for us. And I'd say, I love you too. And I'll miss you. Very much. I'll think of nothing else all day."

Yes you will, Samsa thought. *You'll think of flying the way you never thought of it before, just like I never thought of air until I stopped breathing.*

She shambled towards the kitchen with a spacer's graceless gait, but although she'd always been awkward under gravity, for the first time Samsa thought of a long-forgotten line: "*... as if treading upon knife blades so sharp that blood must flow.*"

She stopped in the doorway, one hand on the jamb, turned to face him. He could see her perfectly well without moving his head, but it seemed right to raise it. She swam into full focus again: porous skin, sagging cheeks; but he could see her, too, all of her. She was so beautiful.

"I'm glad we had this talk," she said, willing a smile. "Have a nice day at work, dear."

Samsa nodded. It was the least he could do. And the most.

The Cool War

In case y'all were wondering how the Berlin Wall came down -- buy me a drink and I'll tell you.

Thank you most kindly, sir. It's good that common courtesy isn't neglected in these dark ages of the 2020's, the way education is --

Speaking of which, what do you know about the Cool War? That we won it? That's it? That's the whole thing?

Sigh. Young people today...

See, there was once a time when the Cool War looked like there was more than one side in it. Russians have always been pretty good at musical warfare. They came late to it; they weren't among the original signers of the Brandenburg Accords in 1724, old Tsar Peter being of the gunpowder-and-bayonet persuasion, but they joined under Catherine, right after she imported half the composers in Italy to her court in Saint-Petersburg. Napoleon almost made Russia regret the choice, having brought the big guns of Beethoven and Rossini, but those used brass wind instruments quite a bit. Ever tried playing "Eroica" outdoors in the winter in Moscow? Poor bastards lost half their orchestra to frostbite. And of course Russians never let anyone forget the time they stopped the Prussians under Wagner with Mussorgsky's "Night on Bald Mountain" while conveniently forgetting the debacle when the whole Russian army ran from a single Austro-Hungarian klezmer quartet before they could deploy for a performance of "1812 overture."

Of course, that was the twentieth century, when it actually mattered whether the people wanted tubas or butter. At least it did among member states of the North Atlantic Touring Orchestra, and vox populi had piped up pretty loud in favor of the dairy industry. The other side was... kinda the way we are now. Soviets started their build-up just as we started the big drawdown, so as our big bands went into early retirement one after another, the Russkis put together division-strength Red Army Chorus units, with mechanized support. We had invested in cutting-edge technology, solid state hi-fi battlefield amplifiers with all-weather loudspeakers, and for a while we had them on the run but then Elvis' enlistment ended, he took "Hound Dog" back Stateside with him, and with that went out hopes for a quick victory. So we settled down to a long, drawn-out, low-intensity war of attrition. We had the advantage of being the more popular side for high-value defectors: Stravinsky, for example -- the Russians never did find a good countermeasure to "Rites of Spring" so they built the Berlin Wall to screen out all the high-pitch dissonances that made it work. They had Paul Robeson for a while, but he was a loose cannon. Every once in a while he sang a song in Yiddish and watched the common soldiers dance and senior officers jump out their windows, so they shut him down. Then he learned enough Russian to figure out some of what they said behind his back and went back to where people at least had the decency to say the same to his face. Their subs would play "Kalinka" at our ships, we'd pipe "Rock Round The Clock" through the SOSUS line, they'd come back with one of their revolutionary songs, like:

> I'm so proud of my Mo-ther-land,
> Workers, peasants walking hand-in-hand,
> From Carpathian Mountains to Bering Sea
> There is no more greedy bourgeoisie...

and we'd respond with "America, oh beautiful."

And so on ad nauseam.

It was into this stalemate that I was commissioned in 1989, a fuzzy-cheeked second lieutenant of violins fresh out of Juilliard, and deployed in my first overseas posting in Berlin at Checkpoint Charlie. I was equally terrified of making a fool of myself in front of my troupe and in front of Bass CO Hollis, and only a little of the enemy. That was dumb, now that I look back on it. The Soviet T-55 Main Battle Trumpet was a scary thing, diesel powered, with a 120 mm smoothbore reed and shaped charge percussion caps; and those Mi-24 Hindemith helicopters could sneak up on you and start playing "Sugar Plum Fairy Dance" as you sat in the latrine -- I get shudders even now, just thinking about it.

But this was Berlin, the war was still cool and occasionally so was the beer, and on our days off we could walk past the checkpoint, flash our military IDs, and stroll right into East Berlin. I loved East Berlin, really I did. It was the only place that could make barracks look bright and shiny and welcoming.

One gray and rainy Sunday I stopped at the PX on my way to Charlie, and ran into my buddy Wes. Wes, it transpired, got one of my brother's letters by mistake, and carried it with him in case he saw me. He slipped it into my pocket, patted my shoulder, and off we went our separate ways. I didn't open it till I got drunk enough to care, at a gray and dingy GDR bar.

There I was, sipping my fifth beer and reading the letter, when I saw the kellner craning his neck to read over my shoulder. He looked like an old Timpanenfuhrer to me, his back hunched from carrying big drums on forced marches, so I turned to bring the letter closer to him, to make him less likely to need a chiropractor afterwards. I heard him tsk-tsk behind me.

"Life is hard in America, no?" he said in a bad movie accent.

I shrugged. "Like everywhere, I suppose," I said.

"Much better here," the koellner said. "We have waltz and you have blues -- there must be reason, nicht?"

I nodded. He spoke again, but damned if I remember what he said, because a blues line crawled into my ear and would not let go, and the words of my brother's letter rearranged themselves into verse:

Went home from work, traffic as far as the eye can see,
I honked my horn, I turned up the AC,
I'm driving so I can't stop at a bar and drink some booze,
I've got the minimum-wage-earning, oppressed-American-worker blues...

The next half-hour was a blur. I remember playing for the kellner and the half-dozen VoPos in the bar on the bar's rinky dink piano:

Woke up this morning, flat tire on my car,
Gotta walk to work, half a mile's too far,
Gonna sweat in the sun, get dust on my shoes,
I've got the minimum-wage-earning, oppressed-American-worker blues...

I remember a crowd gathering, several opening ominous-looking cases to retrieve oboes and bassoons as I sang:

I'm sick of chicken, can't afford filet mignon
more than once a week, how can I go on?
Drinkin' bourbon 'cause I can't afford chartreuse,
I've got the minimum-wage-earning, oppressed-American-worker blues...

I remember marching at the head of a crowd through the streets of Berlin toward the gray, dingy side of the Berlin Wall:

On vacation in Florida, same old sun, same boring palm trees,
Same Atlantic ocean, same Atlantic ocean breeze,
Next year I'll try and save up for a cruise,
I've got the minimum-wage-earning, oppressed-American-worker blues...

And I remember standing in the concrete wreckage, fragmented graffiti iridescent in the sun, taking my bow.

Umm... guys? Where are y'all going?

Pennsylvania Avenue? What's on... Oh.

You can't just sing my song like that, it's copyrighted!

Isaac Newton Failed to Account for Love

On a cold, snowy day in January, as an old Beatles song played on the radio, Joe, whose birthday was in September, had more trouble than usual getting ready for school.

"Eat your breakfast, son," his father said. "Today is, what, French day?"

"In the afternoon," Joe muttered. "Morning is Chemistry." His blush began at his acne and spread to his ears in seconds. "The August group is teaching," he added and hid his face in his toast.

"Joe's got a girlfriend," his brother sang, flashing a gap-toothed smile.

"*Harrumph*," said Joe's father. "Nothing wrong with that, only one month age difference, though of course girls are much more -- mature... at more or less your age..."

"I've had that talk, dad," said Joe. "Three years ago. When I was twelve."

"Oh yeah?" said Joe's father, taking a thoughtful sip of his coffee. "I don't recall talking to you about that."

"You didn't," said Joe. "The March group did."

"I envy our kids sometimes," Joe's mom said.

"Me too," said Joe's dad. He took a step toward the window, cradling his coffee in his hands. "Here they are." He pointed at the park beyond, and at the gaggle of children seated on the grass, an adult teacher a discreet distance away. "Nothing is ever new, you know. Academia was originally an olive garden; Plato would lead students through it --"

"I wish we had cascaded education when we were younger," said Joe's mom.

"The blind leading the blind," Joe's father muttered.

"The young teaching the young, Bob," said Joe's mother. "It works. They learn better, they remember better, with the emotional --"

"Oh, I understand all that," said Joe's father. "What about... What about respect? For elders? For authority?"

"I don't think," said Joe's mother, "that it's any harder to earn than it used to be. Or easier. Now give me a kiss, I gotta go to work."

Joe's father took another sip of coffee, put the cup down on the window sill, and crossed the room to the easy chair where Joe's mother sat, VR helmet in her lap. He leaned over for a kiss that lasted rather longer than absolutely necessary.

"Whew!" said Joe's mom as she broke away. "Good thing my avatar doesn't blush." She slipped the helmet over her head, pausing with the face mask just above her lips so that for a moment, all Joe's dad could see was her smile. He thought of the Cheshire Cat, and made a note to himself to look in Joe's ebook queue to see if he'd ever read ALICE IN WONDERLAND.

"Housecleaning in one minute. OK, postpone, or start now?" the house asked.

Joe's dad crossed the room to sit in an easy chair opposite Joe's mom. "Start now," he said. With a soft hum, floor tiles flipped downward, leaving the furniture standing on the metal grid.

"Look, it's really simple," said Melissa, born on the 13th of August. "Sodium chloride. Sodium has one electron in the outer shell, chlorine seven. Eight is ideal, so sodium gives one up and gets a perfect next-to-last shell, chloride takes it and gets eight, and opposite ions attract. Right?" She looked straight into his eyes, her gaze level and unblinking. Her eyes were so dark they seemed all pupil. Joe drew a breath, with only a small shudder in the middle. Melissa didn't seem to notice.

"A perfect match, right?" he said, trying for that tone he heard a January boy use once, that set a September girl asimper.

"Exactly!" said Melissa and smiled. "Or take iodine with seven and lithium with one. Same thing, right?"

Her smile reached out and grabbed Joe's heart. He'd seen a video of a resuscitation once; what he felt in his chest seemed very close to what defibrillation might be like.

"Right!" he said. "Like this?" He drew a heart on his pad, then another touching it, a plus sign on one, a minus on the other, and sparks flying every which way. The outlines of the hearts came out all wiggly, his hands shaking and all; but the sparks were perfect.

"Well, no," said Melissa slowly.

Even sitting, Joe could feel his knees turn to jelly. "No?" he said hoarsely.

"Think, Joe," she said.

"Right," Joe said. "What about?"

She sighed. "Think back to what we did last week. With eight electrons, chloride would have a filled p-orbital. And lithium with two, that's an s-orbital which is a sphere." She paused. "You see?"

"Right," said Joe. He sketched a shape like two bowling pins stuck together, and a circle next to it.

"Close enough," said Melissa. "Now label the diagram, Joe."

He bent to his tablet again, shielding it from Melissa's view, scribbled furtively, then sat up straight. "Here," he said.

On the tablet, Joe's name was written beneath the bowling pins, *MELITHIUM* across the circle, and like a rainbow above it all stretched flower-strewn, calligraphed *FOREVER.*

Melissa looked up from the tablet. Joe met her gaze, fighting the urge to look away when he saw her expression. The narrowing of her eyes was just like Mom's, last time he didn't pick up his room.

He bit his lip and drew a breath to speak.

Melissa beat him to it. "Joe, there is something I want to tell you," she said.

Joe blinked. "You don't like me?" he said.

"I like you just fine," Melissa said. "But... How do I explain this?"

"You don't need to explain anything," Joe said. "It's OK."

"I'm supposed to be teaching you, aren't I?" she said.

"Yeah," Joe said. "You're supposed to teach me chemistry."

She laughed. "Believe you me, it's all about chemistry." She leaned forward. "It's really next week's material, but... now's as good a time as any." She took the stylus from his hand and drew two diagrams near each other. "This is nitrogen," she said. "Atomic number seven. Two electrons in the s-orbital, three in p-orbital, hybridized." She sketched the waveform quickly. "You see?"

"Yeah, I..." Joe said, and added: "actually, no, I don't."

"It's a different kind of a bond," Melissa said. "Nonpolar covalent. When the two atoms are, mmm, similar. The electrons are shared, not redistributed."

"Yeah?" said Joe.

Melissa nodded. "Yeah," she said.

Joe looked at the diagram again. "N-two," he said. "This is a... covalent bond? Is it as strong as... the other one? Ionic?"

"Actually, it is," Melissa said. "Damn near unbreakable." She smiled and turned to look across the classroom.

Another girl smiled back.

Leah from the June group opened his French textbook. "*Bonjour,*" she said. "*Comment-ca va?*"

Joe sighed. "*Comme ci, comme ca,*" he said.

Leah looked up and raised her eyebrows. "That's going around. Just this morning -- never mind, we have some *Francais* to *parlais,*" she said. "*Aujourd'hui, vous allez revoir les verbes irréguliers.*"

The list rose in his head: to have, *avoir* -- to have a heartache; to want, *vouloir* -- let's not go there; to make, *faire* -- let's *definitely* not go there...

Joe sighed. "To be, *être: je suis -*" *en amour*, he added silently.

Tu es -- tres belle, he realized quite suddenly

Nous sommes -- ici, on a park bench, the scent of honeysuckle and Leah's perfume...

"You forgot third person singular," Leah said. *"Maintenant, répétez avec moi:"*

And in Joe's mind, a fragment of the morning's song rose from its slumber.

"Voulez-vous coucher," he said slowly, *"avec moi?"*

Leah's smile grew larger. *"Ce soir?"* she said, looking in his eyes.

He opened his mouth to speak; for once, he had the perfect reply just in time, and not much later. "Why wait so long?" he tried to say, but no sound came out as he'd forgotten to breathe. He nodded instead.

"L'audace, toujours l'audace," Leah said and blushed.

"How was your day, dear?" said Joe's mom.

"Great," said Joe.

"Learn much chemistry, son?" Joe's father said, winking.

"Sure did," said Joe. "Learned about the two kinds of chemical bonds."

"Oh?" said Joe's mom. "What *are* the two kinds of bonds?"

"Covalent," said Joe, "and ironic."

The Little Dog Ohori

The young soldier jumps to his feet, snaps to attention.

"At ease," the officer says. "And sit down." The officer's shoulders are covered by a white coat; it hides her shoulder tabs, leaving visible only her service branch insignia.

The young soldier hesitates.

"Sit," the officer says. "Because of this --" she lifts her coat momentarily "-- I can make it an order, and because of this --" she points to the caduceus in her lapel "-- I prefer not to."

"Thank you, Comrade Colonel," the soldier says, sees a small frown crease the officer's face, and adds: "I mean, Doctor."

The officer smiles and nods. A strand of graying hair escapes her knot and falls to her face; she sweeps it back with an impatient gesture.

The soldier sits down, and turns toward the hospital bed. He leans toward the dying woman and takes her hand, whispers a word in a language the doctor does not understand.

Cold.

Lying on the riverbank in a puddle of blood and melting snow, she listens for the sounds of gunfire, the roar of engines, the clatter of tank tracks, anything to say she is not alone. She no longer feels her hands, though she can see her right hand on the trigger of her Tokarev-40, the index finger frozen into a hook. She no longer feels pain where the shell splinter tore into her belly, only cold. Cold comfort, too, in the bodies scattered on the ice beyond the riverbank, eleven black specks against relentless white, eleven fewer *Waffen SS* to kill her battalion mates, eleven plus two hundred and three already in the killbook makes --

Oh, what's the difference?

She listens again, and this time there is a friendly sound.

The little dog Ohori is barking.

In her mind, she hears Uncle Tsoi tell the story:

The poor orphan Soo and Ming-De, the yangban's daughter, have loved each other since they were children, and the little dog Ohori loved them both. When the Yangban's greedy heirs plot to get rid of Soo and force the beautiful Ming-De to marry her stepmother's scheming cousin Ko, the little dog saves the orphan boy, and by always being able to find either of the two wherever they are, Ohori brings them together.

The barking stops, but silence does not return. There is a sound like leaves fluttering in the wind.

No, wait. It's winter. Only a white cloak for camouflage. No grass to hide, no leaves to whisper...

Whisper.

"Is she?..."

A woman's whisper, in Russian.

"I don't know."

Another voice, a woman, too, or an angel.

An angel?

There is no such thing as angels, of course, but if you call them they might --

"*Help...*" From a throat parched raw through desiccated lips, one of the last small drops of strength drains into the word, and one more droplet for a thought:

Please, God, if you exist --

-- The darkness deepens --

-- please let me see my family again --

-- a face looks back from the nothingness: Selim's, with his huge happy crooked smile. She tries to reach toward it.

-- please. If only for a moment --

"Were you close, the two of you?" the doctor asks.

The soldier opens his mouth, closes it again. His eyes grow distant, focus far away.

"Sorry," the doctor says. "Stupid of me to ask."

The soldier nods. The doctor takes it as "Yes, we were close," not "Yes, stupid of you to ask."

The woman's breathing is becoming ragged: a burst of rapid gasps, then slow breaths, then rapid again.

"I'm sorry," the doctor says. "It won't be long now."

The soldier reaches into his tunic pocket, brings out a tattered notepad.

"Her diary?" the doctor asks.

"Her killbook," the doctor answers.

"Ah," the doctor says. "I see."

The captain's name, Kryviy, is Ukrainian.

"Age?" he says.

"Nineteen," she answers, a pang of guilt for lying.

"*Natsional'nost'*?" he says.

"Uzbek," she says. A smaller pang.

"Why do you want to enlist?" he says.

This is a question she does not expect. This question wouldn't ever be asked of a man. Or a Great Russian.

She rifles through a list of plausible lies, and settles on a partial truth: "I want to be a sniper."

The captain looks up from his notes. His ice-blue eyes aim at her face. "Sniper?" he says. "Can you see well enough, with those..." He squints in imitation of her features.

She looks out at the sunbaked desert beyond the open window. Some distance away, a truck approaches, raising a plume of dust behind it. She points in its direction.

"Truck number 43-11," she says, and looks at the captain again.

The captain stands up, approaches the window. He watches the truck approach, squints, this time in concentration, and leans out the window.

"I see the 11," he says slowly, then, after a pause: "Yes. 43-11." He returns to his chair, crosses a line off his notes, and writes another. "You'll do," he says, and shouts: "Next!"

She turns to leave, stops for a second at the door. There is a faint barking coming from the window. The little dog Ohori, back from -- wherever they sent Selim?

The woman's hand tightens, just enough to see the tiny twitch. The soldier puts the killbook in her hand. Another twitch.

The doctor leans against the doorjamb. The wood plank creaks. The soldier looks up.

"It took an hour to pry her from that riverbank," the soldier says. "Two nurses from the Medical-Sanitary Battalion. In the dark. Under enemy fire." He shakes his head. "And then they dragged her back to the Division hospital, three kilometers away." He touches his chest; two of his medals ring together. "No matter what I do, I'll never equal what they did, what any one of these three women did."

The doctor's hands are in the pockets of her tunic. Her fingers itch for something – a cigarette, a scalpel – she worries at the knots in the pocket's seam, rolls specks of lint into a ball. *Surgery is easy*, she thinks. *Listening is hard.*

She looks at the kill book. "I'll remember her name. Heroes should never be forgotten."

The soldier raises his head, looks straight at her. She sees the hesitation in his eyes, and the crystallization at a decision.

"That's not her real name," he says slowly, and looks at the dying woman again.

The doctor does, too. She compares the dying woman's features with the soldier's, her trained mind catalogs the differences.

"Korean?" she says. "Passing for..."

"Uzbek," the soldier says quietly.

"Nineteen thirty-seven?" the doctor asks. Matching the soldier's tone comes naturally; suppressing the urge to look behind her for does not.

The soldier looks up. "Not many people know about that."

The doctor says nothing.

"My grandfather was selling lamb samsa at a train stop," the soldier says. "A train of cattle cars stopped there one day. It had been traveling from Siberia for a month."

The doctor's fingers scramble in her pocket. She bites her lip.

"They stopped to bury the dead in the desert. Her mother was one of them. She was thirteen, and an orphan. Grandfather brought her back to our *qishlaq*. She became one of the family."

Selim comes out of the recruiting office, a happy grin on his face.

"I did it!" he says. "They are sending me to sniper school. And I have you to thank."

She draws a breath. "Did you tell them –?"

He shakes his head. "I'm not that stupid. Can you imagine? 'Oh yes, Comrade Captain, a little girl taught me everything I know about hunting.' They would call a neuropathologist next, to have my head examined."

"I am not little, Selim," she says firmly. "I'll be eighteen come spring, and I'll enlist, too. I'll ask to join your unit, and we'll be together again."

His face grows somber. "They won't take you. I'm sorry."

"What are you talking about?" She puts her hand on her hips. "They take girls!"

"They don't take Koreans," he whispers. "They have a list of undesirables: Koreans, Tatars, Volga Germans, Chechens. Only fit for labor battalions."

She does not answer, except for a glint in her eyes: exactly, he thinks, like a glint off the barrel of Grandfather's old Mosin-Nagant .300.

Exactly like the glint she had on the first anniversary of her joining the clan when, returning to the *qishlaq* with an antelope and two hares in the back of their donkey-drawn *arba*, when she turned to him and said, in too-precise Karakalpak Uzbek:

"When I am old enough, Selim, we will be married."

The doctor is used to silences; the soldier is not.

"You might not believe this, but she taught me to shoot," the soldier says.

The doctor says nothing. She reaches for the kill book, turns its pages with reverence.

"What am I saying?" the soldier says. "Of course you believe it, Colonel. Most people --"

"Most people don't command a military hospital," the doctor says. "Most people know what soldiers look like; I've seen what warriors carry inside."

"You must have, as a surgeon," the soldier says.

"That, too," the surgeon whispers.

The train approaches, the smoke from its engine thinning, the chuffing slowing down.

"This makes no sense," says Uncle Tsoi. "First of all, there is no war now; the Japanese were beaten at

Halhin-Gol, and they are not coming back. Secondly, even if they were, why would we help them? We ran away from Korea to get away from the Japanese. And thirdly, why resettle all of us? They could just arrest the richer peasants, like the Pak family." He sighs. "No, I think it's a mistake. I think someone misunderstood what Comrade Stalin said, and when that becomes clear the train will turn around and bring us back here. I just hope it won't be too late for the apple harvest."

He looks up to find that his niece isn't looking at him. She is staring at the train in the distance.

"This isn't polite," Uncle Tsoi says. "You should pay attention when your elders are talking."

She nods absent-mindedly.

"Haven't you ever seen a train before?" Uncle Tsoi says, and follows her gaze.

His face drops. "This isn't a passenger train," he whispers. "We are going to travel ten thousand kilometers in cattle cars."

They wait for the train in silence.

A man approaches, a Great Russian by his appearance.

"Comrade Tsoi?" he calls. "Which of you is Comrade Tsoi?"

Uncle Tsio stands up straighter. "See," he says to his niece. "Someone realized it's a mistake." He turns to the man and raises his hand. "I'm Tsoi," he says loudly.

"Please come with us," the man says softly.

Uncle Tsoi turns to his niece. "Go get your mother."

"Just you," the man says.

The train stops. The gates slide open with a clatter.

"All aboard!" a man shouts from the locomotive.

She watches Uncle Tsoi escorted away from the train, past a line of armed soldiers, until she feels her mother tug at her hand.

She turns. There are tears in her mother's coal-black eyes, rolling down her face that is the palest she had ever seen.

"Come. Have to go," her mother says. A cough escapes before she can cover her mouth.

They board the train in silence, find a spot to sit. More people come until there is no more room. Then some more. Then more.

Then, finally, there is a whistle, the gates clang shut, and the train departs.

"Do you see your target?" Uncle Tsoi says.

Her head tilted over the stock of Uncle Tsoi's Berdan rifle, she gives a tiny nod.

"What are you aiming at?" Uncle Tsoi asks.

"The big pine cone," she says.

"That is wrong," says Uncle Tsoi. "Pick a scale. One scale on the whole pine cone. Aim at that. Have you got that?"

She nods again.

"Now, breathe in, then out, and on the out, close your whole hand on the trigger."

She presses on the trigger, flinching just a bit before the rifle bucks and the shot explodes. The pine cone dances but does not fall.

"Two more things," says Uncle Tsoi. "First, squeeze the trigger slowly enough that the shot comes as a surprise to you. Understand?"

She nods. "And the second?" she says.

"Connect with your target," says Uncle Tsoi. "Some people imagine reaching out and touching it; some talk to the target in their minds. Some apologize in advance for hitting it. You have to care, in some way, about the target, to shoot true.

She aims again, breathes in and out, imagines the little dog Ohori running to the pine tree, leaping to sniff the pine cone, leave a wet print of its nose on one particular scale.

The shot rings out, startling her. The pine cone disintegrates into a cloud of chaff.

Is it a starshell, or dawn already? It is light: light enough to see green grass, birch trees in leaf - it can't be spring - or does it matter? The rhythmic footfalls she hears – pulsing blood, or boots measuring time? And – faces, smiling faces she never thought she'd see again, and voices she never hoped to hear cry, once more, just one more time:

"Hurrah! Hurrah! Hurrah!"

And, nipping at their feet, the little dog Ohori, his barking mixing with laughter and with the shouts of welcome.

The hand gives one more twitch; the chest rises, falls, never to rise again. The soldier frees his hand from her grasp, smoothes her hair, stands up, face to face with the doctor.

"Thank you," he says.

"For what?" the doctor says.

"We got to see each other," the soldier says.

"It's worth so much to you?" the doctor says.

"To me?" the soldier raises his eyebrows. "It does not matter what it's worth to me. It's what *she* wanted. She had been worth a million of me, you know." He pats his pockets, takes out his cap, places on his head, draws to attention and salutes. "Goodbye..." he begins, but then his voice gives out.

The doctor reaches for a carafe on a bedside table, looks for a glass, finds none, and hands the carafe to the soldier.

"Here. Drink from that. Go ahead, drink."

The soldier brings the carafe to his mouth, takes a long swallow.

"Thank you," he says. "And for bringing her here. I know you bent the rules --"

"We take care of our own," the doctor interrupts. "Which includes you. Go get some sleep. Stop by my office in the morning, I'll have my clerk process a leave extension."

The soldier shakes his head. He steps past the doctor through the door, takes another step in the corridor, stops, turns around. "Goodbye, Grandmother," he says. "Give my regards to Grandpa Selim. And to all of your old comrades." He takes a breath. "And a few of mine."

He turns to the doctor. "You see, we, too, take care of our own. There is a unit that's short a man till I come back, and..." he checks his watch "...an Antonov-24 scheduled to lift off for Kandahar in an hour." He draws to attention but does not salute: indoors, without a cap, "one does not lift a hand to honor an empty head," the soldier's mnemonic comes to his mind. "I beg the Comrade Colonel's permission to be dismissed," he says, in crisp militarese.

"Granted," the doctor says, and watches him march away. It isn't lost on her that his cadence is the same as used for change-of-watch before the Monument to the Unknown Soldier.

The doctor waits until she hears his footfalls no more before she covers the old woman's face.

Squiderella

Once upon a time, in a kingdom by the sea, there lived a simple, perfectly normal couple: Squaderella, a noncom in the army of the kingdom, and Squinterella, her wife, exempt from military service due to an unfortunate congenital visual impairment. Their joy, borne of their love for each other, increased tenfold with the birth of their daughter Squiderella; but it was was short-lived, as Squaderella became another casualty of the Cachalot Conflict and Squinterella was left a widow. She was soon courted by Squaleria, a merchant, who had two daughters from a previous marriage: Squawkterella and Squickterella.

Life soon became nearly unbearable for Squiderella. As her mother Squinterella turned a blind eye to Squaleria's machinations, the wicked stepmother evicted Squiderella from her room and forced her to live in the damp, clammy cellar, giving her comfortable bed to her two wicked stepsisters.

"I don't want to share with her," squawked Squawkerella, pointing at Squickterella.

"Eww," said Squickterella.

Squaleria bared her teeth, and silence fell, all arguments cut short.

As time went on, the three girls grew as the adults grew older. As Squiderella outgrew her clothes, she had to wear her stepsisters' castoffs, but none would fit her save a pair of longstockings and eight knee socks, for obvious reasons. What fantasies ran through her head, none can say, but they certainly kept her busy.

One day King's Squire rode up to their door on a bay seahorse. "Hear ye, hear ye!" he bellowed. "The king's two sons are now nubile, and all the maidens of the kingdom are hereby summoned to the Great Ball, so that out of their number brides may be selected!"

"How narrowminded of the King," Squawkterella squawked. "Only maidens?"

"Eww," said Squickterella.

"Shut up!" said Squaleria. "It cuts the competition in half!" And she bared her teeth, ending the argument.

Squiderella was not told of this, for obvious reasons, but she heard the Squire nevertheless, and as her stepsisters fought over finery on sale at the Squander Square department store, she put on her two longstockings and eight knee socks and stole away from the house and to the palace where she hid in a corner, blending into the wallpaper.

Of the beginning of the ball, the less said the better; awkward does not begin to describe it. The King was about ready to call it a night at midnight when, at the first stroke of the tower clock, a stream of water squirted from one corner of the ballroom and extinguished all the candles. Much noise ensued, and, when the candles were relit, they revealed, amid general confusion, both of the princes and eight of the maidens sitting in a circle on the floor with poleaxed expressions and great big caviar-eating grins, and two longstockings and eight knee socks scattered about.

"Double eww, tee, eff," said Squickterella.

"Not fair," squawked Squawkerella.

"Who did this?!" the King thundered.

"I'm telling," squawked Squawkerella, but then Squaleria bared her teeth, cutting her off.

"Nobody's telling nobody nothing," she hissed. "Or else."

Thus it came to pass that the two princes and the eight maidens rode around the kingdom carrying the two longstockings and the eight knee socks to find the person to whom they belonged, never stopping to try them on because everyone they saw could be ruled out immediately, for obvious reasons. At last they stopped before the house in whose cellar Squiderella dwelled.

"Quick!" said Squaleria. "You two get on your hands and knees, I'll put my hands in my pockets and ride you. That's eight plus two. Git!"

"Why do I have to..." squawked Squawkterella.

"Eww," said Squickterella.

Squaleria bared her teeth, cutting the argument short.

Thus they came outside their house, the wicked stepmother riding the two wicked stepsisters.

"What the actual --" said the eight maidens.

"Eww," said the two princes.

But before they could turn around and hoof it back to the palace, Squiderella slithered out of the cellar door, splendid in her nakedness, flashing her chromatophores and wiggling her tentacles, and once again there was no need to try on the two longstockings and the eight knee socks, for obvious reasons. And the two princes, eight maidens, and Squiderella rode off to the palace and lived happily ever after in peace and prosperity because the next time the Cachalot came to invade the Kingdom by the Sea, they saw the princes' and the princesses' caviar-eating grins and turned back in fear that whatever caused them they may be contagious.

The Whale Wore White

My own darling boy,

Two years passed since last I saw you, and yes, I freely admit: it was my fault we parted on less than friendly terms. I paid the price, I learned my lesson. I'm sorry. Please forgive me for leaving you that way – clinging to a coffin in the middle of the storm-tossed sea.

I had my reasons. I was confused, hurt, angry, bewildered, bothered. I hope you understand. I'm different now. I thought things over, I decided what I needed to do. Being a whale of action, I wasted no time dithering. I dove right in, or rather, out.

You've no idea how traumatic it was to come out to my family.

"And what, exactly, is a, how do you say it?" Aunt Dora asked.

"Homosexual," I clicked crisply. "It means I like men."

"What's wrong with that?" asked Aunt Dora. "I like men, too. They are crunchy, and good with seaweed."

"Not that way," I said. "I like men, you know — Carnally."

"That's even better," said Grandpa Tom. "I

remember, one time I rammed the Santa Imelda, she caught fire. Carne asada is a delicacy, too bad we hardly ever see it nowadays. Now, back in the day –"

"I'm in love with a man," I shouted and found myself surrounded by silence. All eyes were on me, but not for long.

"You call yourself a *sperm* whale," my father bit off, his clicks fairly dripping with contempt. With a dismissive, callous flick of a fluke, he turned and swam away, and after him, one by one, all of my kin. My mother departed last, a doleful sigh escaping her blowhole. Her last words to me, rattled off in a querulous whisper: "I always said no good can come of playing with your food."

I knew just what she meant. My first man, many years ago. I do so rue the day I bit off two of his three lower limbs, one of which he after a fashion replaced with a prosthesis made of Cousin Morty's mandible, and the other with a harpoon. Stereotypic, perhaps, but sharp, nevertheless.

I have no family now.

Since then, for seven hundred, threescore and thirteen days I plowed the thunderous solitude of the sea, each day a miserable gray like any other, none but the spineless squid for food, none but the mindless fish for company. I met no other whale of my color, and none that would admit to share my inclinations. *Au contraire.* Many are quite put out by my inquiries. My strength protects me from their teeth, but their sidelong glances, their turning away with a stroke of a tail, most of all their silences wound me deeper than any harpoon could, in the strongest of human hands.

In my loneliness I have come to miss the men who hunted me. I miss their hunger, their hatred. Whatever feelings they harbored toward me were never akin to icy disdain. It is far better to be the object of bloodlust than no lust at all.

I miss the thin old man I crippled, he looked so adorable prancing on the bridge brandishing that phallic object. His harsh words, punctuated by punctures of his weapon, stung me badly. So sorry I let it goad me into that little fit of *pique* in which I sank the *Pequod.* I swear I'll never do so gauche a thing again.

I miss your little tattooed friend. I know you two were close. It gave me a small measure of comfort to see him save your life, though in a fashion none of us could have predicted. You do not know this, but had that ship not hurried to your rescue I would have lent a fin. For, unlikely though it is that I shall ever see you again, your death would have removed even that infinitesimal hope. I doubt I could have lived with that.

I hardly knew the mates, Starbuck and the others, so I cannot say I miss them, but for certain I miss the concept, the Platonic ideal of matehood which they embodied. The luxury of having more than one — of counting them, first mate, second mate, third — it speaks of riches far beyond all pearls and chests of gold I've glimpsed scattered on the ocean's bottom.

So once again I cruise the seven seas, bellowing my call near all shores on which you are likely to stand. Fire Island. Provincetown. Key West. San Francisco Bay. I even swam up the Hudson river to the piers at Greenwich. Many a manly man had given me the eye, but it is you I miss the most. I hope you hear my cry. I hope you answer.

Call me, Ishmael!

Gulliver at Home

We think the aliens are watching all the time. It's safer this way. They don't take kindly to people who upset Dad. Or me.

The aliens don't hold with cruelty.

Dad's eyes are open wide but there's no quiver in his chin, no tears gathering.

"Where are you, Nana?" he says.

"I'm here," I say. "I'm making your lunch."

"Is it ready?" he says.

"Almost," I say.

He paddles to the bathroom, turns on the light. I hear water running, splashing as he washes his hands. He never forgets. His grandma taught him well. He always said I looked like her, moved like her, even smelt like her, ever since I was a little girl, ever since he'd bounced me on his knee as I rubbed my hand over his whiskers, the times he spent his leave at home. And now I cook like her, too, make homemade egg noodles from dough rolled translucent-thin and too much bay leaf in the chicken soup. Once I got that right, there were no more puzzled frowns as he tasted his first spoon of the broth.

Trial and error.

After lunch, as always, he walks over to the library. That was the easy part: he'd recollected the books when he still had his mind, matching editions to memories of his childhood, and shelved each book himself. Now he pulls *Gulliver's Travels*, starts to read. His lips move as he sounds out each word.

Odd how his memory works since aliens brought him back. Or how it doesn't.

My father left for Saturn when I was in sixth grade. He'd been to the Moon more times than he could count, to Mars a few times, missed the Jupiter run but made the Saturn alternate team. His primary broke her leg skiing. Dad got to go, with six other astronauts. His ship broke contact just before the Jupiter slingshot. Two days later, it reappeared in low Earth orbit, with only Dad on board.

With most of Dad, to be pedantic.

☐

The aliens had his childhood home reconstructed: one moment there was nothing, the next, there it was. I still don't know what's more impressive, the speed, or how well it matched Dad's memories. It was a quadrangle with a central courtyard, three storeys high, ground-floor flats with entrances from the yard, all others from balconies that ring the inside walls. He goes out there sometimes, looks at a square of sky, walks round the second-floor balcony, never knocking on any of the doors, never entering the stairwell.

He built a tent several times on warm days, from sheets and clothesline, dragged pillows inside and lay there playing with his toys. I have an old black-and-white photo of him on that balcony; the alien reconstruction is so perfect, I can match the photo exactly to cracks in plaster.

Did aliens get every memory of Dad's? Every last thing he ever saw? Every word he ever exchanged with my mother? Every smell, every taste, every heartache, every joy?

It wasn't hard to love my father, growing up; I rarely saw him. I think my mother loved him, maybe for the same reason. She cried the first time she looked into his eyes and found a stranger looking back; Dad took her hand and whispered, "Why are you crying, lady?" Mom pulled away and ran, sobbing, from the room, and then a while later she tried to come back, but the aliens stopped her. That's pretty impressive, too: one moment she was moving, the next she wasn't.

I wish we knew what the aliens look like.

Some people think my father saved the world. They think the aliens stripped his mind, found it good and decent, and rebuilt it as best they could. They think they left us mostly alone because of what they found in his memories. But what they did to my father, whatever they did to the other six — we still don't know what happened to them — if minds so cold, so ruthless, so

— alien — felt an affinity to my father, what does it say about him?

I wonder about the other astronauts. What fault condemned them?

Gulliver's Travels. My father reads it every day; he never gets past Lilliputians. He read parts of the book aloud to me when I was little, and later I dreamt of being a giant among little people.

Doesn't everyone?

Is everyone cruel to Lilliputians in their dreams?

Or everyone but my father?

Chrestomathy

February 1837, outside St Petersburg

The bullet had no will, only a purpose, and it could not fulfill it alone. There was an eye that sighted along the barrel of the gun (if the bullet could see, it would see the same dark silhouette framed and reflected in the polished smooth bore), a finger that tightened on the trigger, a flint poised above the pan, and a trail of black powder from the pan to the chamber. Above all, there was a man who held the gun, who felt like a god wielding, for the moment, awesome power. Awesome, but not supreme.

The bullet felt no exhilaration (but the man did) as the trigger broke, as the flint fell toward the striker, as the sparks fell to the pan, as the powder caught and flared and burned its way into the chamber, just behind the bullet.

The bullet felt no disappointment as the trace of moisture in the powder slowed its combustion just enough so that the bullet was already moving before the last of the powder flashed into incandescent gas.

The bullet felt nothing at all as it fell to the ice moving just fast enough to bounce a few times, then roll and come to rest inches in front of the boot of the dark man it was meant to kill. It felt no apprehension as the dark man fired back; it felt no guilt as its late owner collapsed into the snow, his blood a scarlet stain that no one saw because a second later it melted through the crust and hid itself from sharply slanting sunlight.

The survivor, oddly, felt nothing for the longest second of his life; then something like pain, as life with which he made his farewell returned like blood to thawing hand, and with it all the thousand natural shocks that flesh is heir to. Of the two men, the survivor was by far the better read. His name was Aleksandr Sergeevich Pushkin; he was thirty-seven years old; he spoke six languages; he was Russia's greatest poet; and he wanted to go home.

That in itself surprised him: he did not want to go to a tavern or a gaming house where at this hour, barely past sunrise, games of hazard would still be going strong amid cups of wine constantly refilled. He did not want to celebrate with old friends or new-minted acquaintances, with long-time mistresses or starry-eyed girls with whom his dark deep hooded eyes, brooding hawklike face dark even in the dead of winter, and quick sardonic wit had irresistible success. He did not have a clever quatrain or a sophisticated sonnet ready to commemorate the occasion.

He only wanted to go home to his wife.

— *The Reluctant Revolutionist*, by Vladimir Nabokov, St Petersburg, 1937

Ulysses-like, the world he wandered,
As his heart ached and his soul bled.
On roads, his horses' hooves had thundered,
On seas, wind whistled overhead.
The Pantheon, the Tow'r of Pisa,
The Sphinx, the Pyramids of Giza,
The stately palaces on Rhine,
The snow and ice in lands Alpine—
He looked without really seeing,
Another sight stayed in his mind:
How Lensky looked at him and died,
As bullet's strike had set him reeling.
— A. S. Pushkin, *The Journeys of Onegin*, London,
1844

Do you not, with each word, each embrace, create
a monster? Not only the child of your body who may
destroy you with unkind words or unjust deeds, but do
you not see the monster looking out at you from the
eyes of every man you kiss? Do you not hear his roar in
the words of contrition from every servant you upbraid?
I curse Frankenstein not for creating me; I curse him
for being a man, for men create things, and women
beings. Were I of a woman created, no one could call me
a thing.
— Mary Wollstonecroft Shelley, *Heir of
Frankenstein*, London, 1846

"What I will tell you, no one yet knows," Pushkin said. "In truth, there's much I do not understand."

Gogol shrugged. "There's very little in life of which I can claim comprehension. Tell me if you wish; I will not judge."

"The night before the duel I went to the Kazan Cathedral," said Pushkin, "I thought a prayer there might help me as it helped our soldiers before they faced Napoleon's horde."

Gogol nodded, recalling the oft-repeated tale.

"There was a beggar on the steps," Pushkin continued. "She seized my coat; I felt her shiver and reached for a kopeck in my pocket. She took it and looked into my eyes. 'I see your fate,' she said, and sang:

'Muscina, zhenshchina, svinets,
Ot nih pridet tebe konets'."

"*Bozhe moi,*" exclaimed Gogol. "My God! 'Man, woman, lead/Of them you will be dead?!' To hear this before a duel—you must have..."

"I felt no fear," Pushkin interrupted. "Fear is for those who have doubts. I knew I would die, there was no reason to worry; even the little hope I had that caused my heart to flutter now and then when I considered D'Anthes' reputation—even that was gone.

Fear is a colt by Doubt out of Hope, and neither had been present in my stable by the morning."

Pushkin's words came quickly, as if untold the memories fermented to a pressure such as no champagne cork ever held back. In giving memories voice he also gave them leave:

"The sleigh ride to the river, the seconds' words, the pacing off—these I do not remember; but I will never forget the black, malevolent eye of D'Anthes' pistol erupt in fire. Yet nothing struck me. I raised my pistol and fired at once. For a moment I thought I missed too; then D'Anthes sank slowly to his knees."

Pushkin paused to regain his breath.

"The homeward journey took me along Nevsky Prospekt, past the same cathedral. The mad beggarwoman was gone; the morning light suffused the cupola, sparking off the gilded dome, and, though undoubtedly alive, I could not rid me of the thought that the prophesy was true, and so remained."

Gogol crossed himself, a quick Ukrainian gesture rather than the broad, slow Russian one.

— *The Reluctant Revolutionist*, by Vladimir Nabokov, St Petersburg, 1937

I have many times attempted to write my great-grandfather's story, yet its plain facts are so fantastic as to seem a delirious dream when plainly put down. My great-grandfather, a Negro named Abraham

Hannibal, whose born name and true ancestry are forever lost, was given in his youth as a gift to Tsar Peter the Great during his journey to Constantinople. The Tsar arranged for his education, in arts, sciences, languages, and military affairs. Abraham first married a woman who loathed him, at the command of his Sovereign, then a German princess who loved him at the command of his heart. He rose in the military service to the rank of General-En-Chef, and was given a patent of nobility and a village of serfs by the Empress Catherine as a reward for meritorious service. At his death, one of his sons was an admiral. In my native country, the story is known to everyone and would surprise no one; but as many times as I told it in English I have received wide-eyed looks that I am certain were reserved for Bedlamites.

At Invalides in Paris I found the records of his education as an infantry officer; the fortress of Narva stands as he built it on Russia's western border; on the island of Navarone, his son's daring landing in the Turkish wars is remembered; my great-grandfather was not imagined by me, as Onegin, the Russian everyman, had been, and yet only now am I able to write his tale.

— A. S Pushkin, *The Moor of Peter the Great*, London, 1845

July 1838, Via Sistina, Rome

"I can never go home again," said Pushkin.

Nikolai Vasilievich Gogol nodded with understanding. "I have heard... Letters, traveling acquaintances stopping by... Your wife, running to D'Anthes' deathbed, crying in public at his funeral..."

"I opened my door," Pushkin said. "Natasha ran to me. She was frightened. I thought she was frightened for my safety. She searched my face, and then I watched as her own face—melted and recast itself into a mold I'd never seen before, a mask of—hatred, and anger, and—of disappointment. She threw on a coat and started pulling on her boots. I don't know why I felt I had to apologize. I muttered something about having better luck while he was the better shot. 'He was the better man,' my wife shouted, slamming the door. Later in the day, friends came. The Tsar was heard to mutter something that amounted to 'Will no one rid me of this tiresome blackamoor?' And here I am, a blackamoor who no longer has a home. Warsaw, Berlin, Amsterdam, Paris—all places are the same to me now. Rome, too; perhaps a better place than most, since you are here."

"If there exists a country in the world in which suffering, sorrow, death and one's own impotence are forgotten, that place is Rome: what would become of me elsewhere?" said Gogol, waving his arms as always when making a pronouncement, hyperbole attending his speech as subtlety his writing. "Italy is mine! No one can take it away from me. I was born here. Russia, St. Petersburg, snow, scoundrels, teaching the theatre: that was all a dream. I woke up anew in my homeland."

Pushkin turned to look about the room, its window facing west catching at last the rays of setting sun. Gogol's squalid, airless chamber belied his praise. The smallest gap between the shutters let in a shaft of light that, having sparked the plentiful dust suspended in the air into a faerie incandescence, struck the papers on Gogol's desk like a frozen thunderbolt. Unlike the rest of the room, hidden in murk, the half-completed page shone with reflected light as Gogol's words upon it, in cramped Cyrillic hand, shone with his brilliance.

"Dead Souls," Gogol said. "You gave me the idea to write it, back in St Petersburg, but it has since then taken a life of its own. I see the characters, speak to them, they answer back; it is like *The Inspector General* all over again, but I'm afraid no one will ever read it. I don't know if it will get past the censors; it was a close run for *Inspector*, and it hardly even mentions souls—slaves, that is. Sometimes—"

Gogol stood motionless, his sad wet eyes looking at Pushkin, arms at his sides as when he told the bare unembroidered truth—"Sometimes I despair. And I have no wish to return. It is not possible for beautiful souls to live in Russia, only pigs can keep their heads above water there," he said, raising his hands. "But, mostly, I am happy. In Rome, my soul is luminous. I am working and I try with all my strength to bring my book speedily towards its end. Life, life, a little bit more life!"

"A little bit more life," Pushkin said slowly. "What words can be more fitting for my own device?"

— *The Reluctant Revolutionist*, by Vladimir Nabokov, St Petersburg, 1937

With that Plunkett donned his spectacles, and once more started to rummage in the cupboard, and to smother his guest with dust as he untied successive packages of papers—so much so that his victim burst out sneezing. Finally he extracted a much-scribbled document in which the names of the deceased slaves lay as close-packed as a cloud of midges, for there were a hundred and twenty of them in all. Chester grinned with joy at the sight of the multitude. Stuffing the list into his pocket, he remarked that, to complete the transaction, it would be necessary to return to the town.

"To the town?" repeated Plunkett. "But why? How could I leave the house, seeing that every one of my servants is either a thief or a rogue? Day by day they pilfer things, until soon I shall have not a single coat to hang on my back."

"Then you possess acquaintances in the town?"

"Acquaintances? No. Every acquaintance whom I ever possessed has either left me or is dead. But stop a moment. I do know the banker. Even in my old age he has once or twice come to visit me, for he and I used to be schoolfellows. Yes, him I do know. Shall I write him a letter?"

"By all means."

"Yes, him I know well, for we were friends together at school."

Over Plunkett's wooden features there had gleamed a ray of warmth—a ray which expressed, if not feeling, at all events feeling's pale reflection. Just such a phenomenon may be witnessed when, for a brief moment, a drowning man makes a last re-appearance on the surface of a river, and there rises from the crowd lining the banks a cry of hope that even yet the exhausted hands may clutch the rope which has been thrown him—may clutch it before the surface of the unstable element shall have resumed for ever its calm, dread vacuity. But the hope is short-lived, and the hands disappear. Even so did Plunkett's face, after its momentary manifestation of feeling, become meaner and more insensible than ever.

— *Dead Souls*, by N. V. Gogol and Edgar Allan Poe. Richmond, Virginia, 1850

The fear in the man's eyes was a sight familiar to me; yet, where others had fled with this fear, or attacked me with it, the black-skinned man did neither. He fell to his knees before me. "Oh, help me, help me," he cried, over and over. In the woods there appeared first a straw hat and a musket tip, and presently a man bearing both appeared from behind the briars. The black man turned; the fear was obviously directed at the newcomer. The latter unslung his musket and aimed at me. I looked back, unafraid. Having been wounded before, with less reason, the musket-ball tearing my flesh held no terror for me.

— Mary Wollstonecroft Shelley, *Frankenstein Unchained*, Richmond, Virginia, 1849

1848, Brontë household, Branwell's funeral
Upon the curate a frightening change had come. He held a hunting gun with hands as firm and as implacable as his face, his stance speaking of intimate familiarity with the weapon. It occurred to me that, as targets, we were far larger than grouse, and far less mobile.

"Next one who moves is dead," Mr Brontë said. "I buried my son today. You'll not be taking my daughters."

We stopped. We stood in silence for what seemed an eternity. Then Pushkin raised his hands and stepped forward. "You only have one shot, Patrick," he said gently, "Yet with it you could take four lives. Look, sir, at your daughters. Look: what pale, thin, barely living wraiths they have become upon these pestilent moors; they'll not survive the winter. If slake you must your anger, shoot me, sir; I'll gladly join your son in Yorkshire ground, if such is my destiny, but I pray, sir: let thy daughters go. I see in every one of them such greatness as few dream of. Shoot me, and let them have...a little bit more life."

I stepped forward at these words. "Pushkin speaks wisely, Reverend," I said. "Mark his words, I pray."

"What can he do?" said Mr Brontë bitterly. "Set against Fate, what can one man do?"

"What if it's Providence," I said, "that brought us here?"

The longest second of my life was spent in contemplation of the levelled gun ere its barrel descended.

— Mary Wollstonecroft Shelley, *Journeys and Peregrinations*, Richmond, Virginia, 1850

"Everything has been carried through in due form!" he cried. "The man whom I mentioned is a genius indeed, and I intend not only to promote him over the rest, but also to create for him a special Department. Herewith shall you hear what a splendid intellect is his, and how in a few minutes he has put the whole affair in order."

"May the Lord be thanked for that!" thought Chester. Then he settled himself while the Colonel read aloud:

"'After giving full consideration to the Reference which you had entrusted to me, I have the honour to report as follows:

"'(1) In the Statement of Plea presented by one Paul Chester, Gentleman of Virginia, there lurks an error, in that an oversight has led the Petitioner to apply to Revisional Slaves the term "*Dead.*" Now, from the context it would appear that by this term the Petitioner desires to signify *Slaves Approaching Death* rather than *Souls Actually Deceased*: wherefore the term employed betrays such an empirical instruction in letters as must, beyond doubt, have been confined to the Grammar School.'

"The rascal!" Calhoun broke off to exclaim delightedly. "He has got you there, Mr Chester. And you will admit that he has a sufficiently incisive pen?

"'(2) It shall therefore be recorded that in the county of Gorman there now reside 10,124 slaves owned by Mr Chester, whether Approaching Death or Otherwise; for the reason that all Negroes shall be counted as three fifth of a white man, according to Article 1 Section 2 sub 3 of our Constitution, the population of the County of Gorman now stands at 7,143 for the purposes of the Census of 1840, the said County has not enough persons to become a Virginia Congressional District."

"Why did you not tell me all this before?" cried Chester furiously. "Why you have kept me dancing about for nothing?"

"Because it was absolutely necessary that you should view the matter through forms of documentary process. This is no jest on my part. The inexperienced may see things *subconsciously*, yet is imperative that he should also see them *consciously*."

But to Chester's patience an end had come. Seizing his cap, and casting all ceremony to the winds, he fled from the house, and rushed through the courtyard. As it happened, the man who had driven him thither had, warned by experience, not troubled even to take out the horses, since he knew that such a proceeding would have entailed not only the presentation of a Statement of Plea for fodder, but also a delay of twenty-four hours until the Resolution granting the same should have been passed. Nevertheless the Colonel pursued his guest to the gates, and pressed his hand warmly as he thanked him for having enabled him (the Colonel) thus to exhibit in operation the proper management of a census. Also, he begged to state that, under the circumstances, it was absolutely necessary to keep things moving and circulating, since, otherwise, slackness was apt to supervene, and the working of the machine to grow rusty and feeble; but that, in spite of all, the present occasion had inspired him with a happy idea—namely, the idea of instituting a Committee which should be entitled "The Committee of Supervision of the Committee of Management," and which should have for its function the detection of backsliders among the body first mentioned.

— *Dead Souls*, by N. V. Gogol and Edgar Allan Poe. Richmond, Virginia, 1850

April 5. —I am almost devoured by *ennui*. Pundit is the only conversible person on board; and he, poor soul! can speak of nothing but antiquities. He has been occupied all the day in the attempt to convince me that the ancient *Amriccans* governed themselves! —did ever anybody hear of such an absurdity? —that they existed in a sort of every-man-for-himself confederacy, after the fashion of the 'prairie dogs' that we read of in fable. He says that they started with the queerest idea conceivable, viz.: that all men are born free and equal— excepting the Negro slaves, of course—this in the very teeth of the laws of gradation so visibly impressed upon all things both in the moral and physical universe. Every man 'voted', as they called it—that is to say, meddled with public affairs—until, at length, it was discovered that universal suffrage gave opportunity for fraudulent schemes, by means of which any desired number of votes might at any time be polled, without the possibility of prevention or even detection, by any party which should be merely villainous enough not to be ashamed of the fraud. A little reflection upon this discovery sufficed to render evident the consequences, which were that rascality must predominate—in a word, that a republican government could never be anything but a rascally one. With this Pundit readily agreed, saying that after only fourscore and ten years of such foolishness *Amriccans* lit upon another scheme of government, to wit: each slave owner would elect a slave and send him to the government; and the slaves would govern, and each week all free white men would vote on whether the governors would be rewarded, with molasses cakes and whisky, or whipped; at which I wondered aloud why we see no evidence of *Amriccans* in the world today, for a government so organized should last an eternity.

 — Edgar Allan Poe, *Mellonta Tauta*, Richmond, Virginia, 1851

 There is no question but that slavery is enshrined in our Constitution; yet the intent of our Founding Fathers is clear from their injunction against slave trading after 1808. Slavery had been an economic necessity in those difficult times, but the Founding Fathers foresaw, indeed desired, its end.

 The Founding Fathers did not usurp to themselves the infallibility that, by rights, belongs to Providence alone. The falsehood of their opinion of the Negro as an unfortunate race fit for slavery and no more has been amply demonstrated. There are, indeed, persons for whom slavery as a way of life is the only reasonable condition, but this can hardly be determined either from the circumstances of their birth or from the color of their skin.

It is the opinion of this court that, by his actions, Mr Dred Scott has amply demonstrated his intelligence and his respect for the law. It is therefore clear that he does not conform to the definition of slave; that, indeed, the word "slave" had been to him erroneously applied. Thus he does not require manumission. Furthermore, only those persons, of any race, who desire to enter, or remain in, the condition of slavery, may be said to be in the condition of servitude. It is beyond the intent of the framers of our Constitution for us to expound on the equitable means of revision of their status, and we shall leave that to the several States of this Union.

— Chief Justice Roger B Taney, Majority Opinion in DRED SCOTT vs SANDFORD, 1856

"In this enlightened age, there are few I believe, but what will acknowledge, that slavery as an institution, is a moral & political evil in any Country. It is useless to expatiate on its disadvantages. I think it however a greater evil to the white man than to the black race, & while my feelings are strongly enlisted in behalf of the latter, there are many whom I counted among our friends who abhor the recent Ruling of the

Supreme Court to the point of inciting Rebellion. However, there are, in addition to myself, many among the formerly staunch advocates of slavery who will now readily affirm that an end to this Institution is necessary in order to form a more perfect Union."

— Lt Col Robert E Lee, in a letter to his wife, 1856

Arlington, 1870

"Come in, Senator," said Custis. "Father should be glad to see you."

I had never before been this close to a man who survived an apoplectic fit. I had seen tears, pain, wounds, but it was the sight of Robert's half-smile, and his good left hand cheerfully waving to me, that reduced me momentarily to tears. I walked over and sat at his side. I clasped his immobile right hand, as friends do; his left swept over to cover and squeeze mine. The stroke, it seemed, made of him two men: the left side of his face was flaccid, its features hanging in a mask of profound sadness, left eye, unable to close, leaking tears that tracked into his beard. Custis came to the other side of his wheelchair—Martha's wheelchair, now carrying its second rider—and carefully wiped the trail of tears. He then swept his hand over the General's eyelid, closing it to spread the tears over the whole eye.

General Lee, never a voluble man, was silenced by his malady. The right side of his face carried on its campaign of welcoming me, even though no help from the left flank or the tongue in the center could be expected. He was too good a soldier to give up while any strength remained at his command.

"You knew, General," I whispered. Out of the corner of my eye, I saw Custis nod. "You knew, and planned accordingly."

Custis cleared his throat. "Father divested from all of his stock in steam companies a month ago. I heard you did, too, Senator."

Steam companies. What wonders have they wrought! I had been for some time aware of a cool breeze in the room, quite startling on a sultry September afternoon in a house with all windows tightly shut. It did not quite surprise me, as in my home in New Orleans I had a similar device. One shovels coal and pours water in one end; and cold air blows from the other. Robert, a soldier-engineer, could in better days have explained its workings to me; I, a mere lawyer, was content to use it without much thought. The steam train brought me to Washington in a day and a half; the steam car took an hour's drive to Arlington; steam tractors drew harvesters through the fields on both sides of my route; steam ships waited in the harbors we passed and floated under bridges we crossed; steam engines turned generators that made the electricity on which our telegraphs ran; steam armored chariots defended our borders. As for the stocks—they soared as money chased after every inventor who purported to find new use for steam or new method of its generation, till a hundred years of dividends would not buy back its purchase price. This was the state of affairs that ended but a fortnight ago. Smart money divested first; the market crashed as other money followed.

"When you chose me for running mate," I continued, "I was among those who questioned your sanity. So many good men—Davis, Seward, Grant... With any one of them you could have had a fighting chance at the White House, even against Fremont and Lincoln, popular incumbents in the midst of great prosperity in which this country found itself after the first four years of their Presidency. Yet you chose me. Now I understand. You knew of two things that could not last another four years: your health, and the prosperity. You did not wish to be remembered for infirmity in office and a disaster in economy. Yet there was one thing more you wished to add to your distinguished legacy: one more race for which you would win acceptance and full rights in law and in everyday life. And every vile slur that was thrown at us, was by their perpetrators remembered, and rebounded upon them this very month."

"So you understand," Custis said, and Robert once again squeezed my hand. "Father knew you would."

I shook my head. "He thought too highly of me. As I left New Orleans I was still unenlightened. It was only as I stepped off the train in Washington that my epiphany came, and I knew that undefeated General Lee's final battle plan had borne its fruit."

The General's hand fluttered once again, the half-smile grew, bidding me to continue. I drew a great breath and continued:

"I passed a man sitting on a bench, reading the *New York Post*. His clothes spoke of former affluence, now much reduced. As I walked behind him I heard him mutter: 'I should'a voted for the Jew'."

— Judah Benjamin, *Memoirs*, New Orleans, 1874

New York, 1876
My dear Emily,
Man, woman, lead...

I think at last the prophesy is coming true. Having outlived my friends, and reached the age of seventy-seven, and finding myself somewhat enfeebled, I sought counsel of a physician. He sent me to a colleague to be "scoped."

I cannot tell which was the greater wonder: the scoping machine, buzzing and crackling with power, a screen that glowed when power was applied; or the doctor—the woman doctor! —who, having donned a coat that appeared so heavy I could hardly credit her staying upright under it, proceeded to turn me this way and that, seeing on the screen my ribs, my heart, and— the disease of which I will die. I am the man, the doctor is the woman, and her coat is made of lead, to protect her from the power of her machine. Man, woman, lead...

I am ready; there is, at last, no question of escaping fate, through still I have 'a little bit of life'. I have had my forty-year reprieve; I lived as best I could; I but regret how little I accomplished. As for what time remains, I plan to spend it well. First, a stop at Mary's grave—oh would she were here to see these wonders!; then—you know me well enough. If only you were here...

— A. S. Pushkin, letter to Emily Brontë, 1876

The melancholic Gogol, the alcoholic Poe, the consumptive Brontës, the grieving Shelley: all acknowledged a debt to Pushkin for bringing them back from the brink of death; all are acknowledged to have written their finest works under Pushkin's influence. And each became a voice in the Great Reflection, an awakening of the American national conscience, a renewal of the American spirit.

My own homeland is not only the source of this renewal, but also its beneficiary. I am of the opinion that it was under the influence of American events that Tsar Alexander II abolished serfdom and established constitutional monarchy on the British model, all within barely a year of his coronation. Were the monarchy still absolute at Alexander II's death, one shudders to think what Alexander III, his demented son, would have done to my beloved country.

The dour, humourless Marx is surely sneering at these words from his grave: he who believed that slavery died a natural death, of industrial impotence and economic inefficiency. To which I say: were any institution's life measured by its economic efficiency, we writers should have long become extinct.

— *The Reluctant Revolutionist*, by Vladimir Nabokov, St Petersburg, 1937

On D'Anthes' coffin lay and sobbed my wife:
She cried for me as much as for her love:
One lay below ground, one walked above,
And happy never would be either's life.
I was condemned to walk the Earth and grieve
Till I could him, her, and myself forgive.
— A. S. Pushkin, *For Mary*, Richmond, Virginia, 1876

1877, New York
You have asked me, Your Honor, if I am sorry for what I done, and to that I must answer, without a doubt, yes. I am indeed most powerfully sorry. You heard, as did the gentlemen of the jury, my attorney as he recounted my humble origins and my need to feed my family when I was but a child myself. Grown up on

a farm, I knew from boyhood all there is to know about livestock, and my first fortune I earned in the slave trade. I bought and sold and bought and sold until I have some thousand and more prime field hands, and then one day wasn't nobody wanting to buy them no more on account of it was not done in the high society to own slaves and everyone was selling theirs. So I turned them all loose, gave them their freedom even before Damned Scot, didn't keep but three house wenches as I was broke—and damme to hell if all three didn't up and run off the minute they found out slavery wasn't no more.

So, like I said, sorry I was that I ever traded slaves as this got me poor and nobody wanted anything to do with me for a long time after. But I did know horses and mules, could ride them like the wind and had the eye for colts and fillies that'd be worth something growed up and all, so I went into the horse trade and pretty soon had me a thousand head or more and an order for all them to be paid in gold by the United Goddam States Goddam Army—and then Washington decides not to chase Redskins around the Territory no more and to keep to the Indian treaties and all my horses are of no use to nobody and I turned them loose on the prairie, same as my slaves. Powerfully sorry I am that I ever believed the US government would deal straight with a man like myself.

Then, seeing as all the things horses and men used to do, steam is doing now, I invested in steam company shares, and y'all know how that came out, no need to tell.

So I went to New York and started a nice business selling fake British passports to Irishmen, seeing as the quota favored the English and they would have an easier time of it immigrating with papers from a civilized country, had myself a thousand or more of the best quality fake passports made, when Washington repeals the quota and lets the Irish into the country like they was white people and I got no buyers for the passports and I'm broke again.

And I sure don't do much reading—hardly any, past what I need for my business—but I hear from people how there are these writers writing books that make fun of right-thinking white Americans like myself and making us like the demons and the Abolitionists like the angels, making things all upside down in peoples' heads till they don't know which end kisses and which end pisses. I don't know who these people are, but I surely do know who my wife is, she's the girl that was sixteen when her family gave her to me in trade for a stack of passports they hadn't any money to buy and is now twenty and the purtiest Irish redhead you ever—sorry, Your Honor—

Anyhow, Your Honor, when I came back to my rooms after a day of seeking employment fit for a white man of fifty-five years old, and found my wife in my bed and not with me and not alone, neither, you can't expect me to be sorry for taking out my Colt and plugging whoever don't belong in there. But sorry I am, and powerful sorry I am, that I did not know who that was who turned to me and smiled all sweet when he saw my gun on him; for if I had known that gray old man was a Negro and if I had known he was one of that nest of troublemakers that ruined my life at every turn, I would not have put the first bullet between his eyes, no sir; I had a six-shooter and most sorry I am that I did not use all six to make it more entertaining, and that's the truth, Your Honor, so help me God, or my name ain't Nathan Bedford Forrest.

Don't Look Down

My body remembers what I can't.

My hands move to the sides, legs move apart, knees bend.

A whistling in my ears: wind. It's called wind. I'm flying, flying in the wind, under the blue that's called the sky, toward the brown that's called the ground. I feel it push my hands, my legs, my face. I feel a weight against my back. Pack? Heavier by the second. "Ten, nine, eight..."

Mate. Late. Fate. Foot. Boot.

Shoot.

Para-chute.

A figure flies into my sight. She waves her hand. She is wearing gloves. She loves. She loves me.

Of course she loves me, she is my daughter!

The sky is blue, the sun is bright, the ground is brown. I close my eyes and all is white where memories should be. What is that droning noise? "De plane, Boss!"

White suit. White dress. Wedding.

Glasses. Rings. "To have, to hold, till dying do us part."

A man steps out of the white: black hair. A smile. And boots. Boots on the ground. Combat boots. Combat drop. Black op.

Stop.

Eyes open. Blue, brown, bright. My daughter who loves me is wearing gloves. A parachute. A helmet. A helmet is hard.

"Dying is easy. Comedy is hard."

"Is that a crash helmet?"

"Oh, I hope not!"

To crash: to hit the ground with a sound.

The ground is brown. It's coming close.

Eyes close.

My daughter looks out of the white. Her face is wet. With water? Not water, tears. Fears? "What if you forget?" she says. "In your condition, what if you can't remember--?"

"Then that's the day," I hear myself say, "that should go on my gravestone. I won't be living then, just postponing the..."

Funeral.

Black dress. Black hole in the ground. My daughter's tear-wet face. Amazing Grace. "How sweet the sound!"

Mound.

"I'm sorry for your loss," I hear someone say. "He was my friend."

He was.

Eyes open.

My daughter is not in front of me. I look up, and there she is, above me, parachute open, floating away.

My hand remembers: a tiny hand in mine, warm. Squirm. Pull away. Run. Black hair waving in the sun. Toward a building.

School. Pull?

Wind pushes on my --

Breast.

My breast remembers: A tug of lips, a flow of milk. A warm squirming welcome weight. A quiet peace.

My body remembers joy, and a memory of a memory of pain.

My hand remembers.

It reaches for the ring.

Pull.

A tug, then an absence of sound.

Don't look down at the ground.

#

We walk, my daughter and I, toward a thing that's glass on top and brown all over. My feet remember, and I walk toward one side, but then my daughter takes my hand and leads me to the other. She opens the door. I sit. My back remembers the seat. My hand remembers a ring, pulls it down to a snap. Strap! The thing will go fast. We have to go far.

Car!

My daughter sits beside me. Wipes a small water from her face.

"I thought I'd lost you," she says.

"I can't be lost," I say. "I'm here."

She seems to laugh, but why is there more water?

"Can we go again?" I say.

She does the thing to make it dry. "A month from now," she says. "As usual. OK?"

"OK," I say. I think I heard her say the same thing, once before. Or more than once.

She steps on something, and we go. Bright sun ahead, brown dust behind; and all above us, a blue dome.

We go home.

Tempora Mutantur

April 1, 2848

In her haste to depart the Scottish Hislands before the start of the monsoon season, the *Starling* set sail before all my luggage had arrived, and I found myself constrained to embark without my books or toiletries. It is fortunate that I have Pundit for my cabin-mate; he is seemingly prepared for every exigency, and his collection of papers on the Savage Continent is like nothing I have ever seen. And--a most agreeable surprise--he speaks not only Swahindi and the tribal Anglic dialects, but my native language as well! The long voyage before me seems less tedious already for his presence.

I have also made acquaintances among the crew. Where other men may fear heights or small enclosed spaces, my own irrational dread is of anthropophagy, and I endeavored to make certain that the ship is amply provisioned against becalming or marooning. The Captain has informed me that the seas along our route are teeming with fish, and victualing is among the least of his concerns. I find this most reassuring.

April 15

The *Starling* has all sails to the wind, but even so, barely makes six knots, and I am sick of mackerel for breakfast. Worse yet, I am almost devoured by ennui, so much so that I had to fight the temptation to jump overboard during our lengthy transit of the coast of Greenland. The dreams of cavorting with half-naked native women in the shade of palm trees might have got the better of me; were it not for the crocodiles that are said to infest the shallows, I should have swam to shore right there and then, and to perdition with my duty to science. The nightmares, however, of the long, sharp, daggerlike saurian teeth tearing my flesh have kept me firmly ensconced in my stifling cubicle.

Pundit, bless his soul, has his documents to occupy his attention, the lucky so-and-so. He reads Anglic better than anyone in the world, though no one is sure how anything was pronounced by the ancients, to whom his documents refer as *Amrikans*, while I of course know them as *Umrikantsi*. Pundit throws around terms like "*elision*" and "*epenthesis*" to explain his theories, to wit: that the key to understanding lost civilizations lies in the painstaking analysis of toponyms and ethnonyms.

In light of this it seems a foregone conclusion that the natives of the Savage Continent were so feared by their neighbors that their very name was derived from the same Indo-European root, *mri-*, as the Slavic "*Umri*", or Latin "*memento mori.*" I inquired upon the possible derivation of the suffix, but Pundit informed me that a firm consensus has yet to be reached. On the one hand, *"Kanuks"* were the *Amrikans'* neighbors to the north, and *"killers of Kanuks"* is one possible etymology. On the other hand, Pundit was of course aware that in my own language, Parusski, the name parses as: *"Umri"*, which is "die" in the imperative mood, and *"Kantsi"*, or "ends." *"Die and be done with it?"* An odd connotation, that, but then nothing about the *Amrikans* makes sense.

Pundit has shared with me a further, more fanciful, theory, which nevertheless has some adherents in Academia, to wit: that *"kan"* refers to cannibalism, of which the natives were often accused. Having recovered from a momentary swoon, I hastened to point out to him that this accusation is only to be found in texts written by their adversaries, and should therefore be taken with a modicum of skepticism. Pundit agreed with this, but reminded me that no written records have survived that show the least scinitlla of friendliness to *Amrikans*; perhaps they had no friends but only slaves and enemies. In any event, one should not readily accept the opinions even of contemporary writers without additional evidence, and it will fall to me to search for such evidence once we reach our destination. As to that, the captain has not committed to a definite timetable: it may take a week if the wind freshens, a month if not.

April 17

Pundit has been busy translating the names of the lost cities, and inscribing them on the great map for our edification. One that drew my attention in particular is the remarkably well-preserved seaside resort, Whore-Land-of, which, regrettably, lies far to the south of our destination.

April 20

Great news! We have gained a following wind, and the Desert Shore is in sight. The Captain has consulted his astrolabe and altered course lest we strike bottom on the shoals of Boss-Town, or reefs off Rod Island. The Gulf of Broke-Land is now no more than a few days sail away!

As Pundit subjects each map notation to his linguistic analysis, it amazes me how even the names of the *Amrikan* cities reflect their violent past. The Gulf is surrounded by the ruins of Bayonne (no doubt the birthplace of the bayonet) and Hack-and-Sack, and further to the south lie the remains of War-Sing-Town, the ancient capital, where the Great Spear was found. It seems harder and harder, each day, to dismiss the first-hand accounts of *Amrikans* as bloodthirsty, rapacious savages.

April 23

We have dropped anchor! Where but a week ago I deplored the windless calm, I now welcome it. The waters off Broke-land are calm and crystal clear, at noon the light reaches the bottom, some fifty meters below. Already I can see--or at least imagine--the outlines of buried treasure in the contours of the sediment. One final day of preparatory tedium; tomorrow, we dive!

April 26

The dig is slow enough to drive one to distraction; there are not enough diving bells, or sailors to man the pumps. I spend as much time as I can at the bottom, trying to disturb the sediment as little as possible. We can only count on ourselves, and the supplies we brought: this desert shore has not been touched by human feet in years, and rain in centuries.

Back in the day, however, it seems this was a great port city. We have uncovered pieces, apparently of a great idol that once stood at the mouth of the harbor. Just to the North of the slave pens at Hell-is Island we found a granite pedestal in the shape of a *shiruken*; near it, a bare foot,and a hand clutching the hilt of a broken *katana* sword. Of greatest interest is a fragment of a stele, with a well-preserved inscription in Anglic. It will be the very first piece I shall bring up, for Pundit's perusal.

April 27

I am seized by dire forebodings and apprehensions.

Pundit has been most helpful in deciphering the partial inscription. At first I thought it was quite the sort of thing one has come to expect from Amrikans, a demand for slaves:

"Give me your tired, your poor, your huddled masses..."

What I cannot reconcile with what we know of the Amrican character--their well-attested brutal efficiency--is the desire this inscription professes for inferior workers or indifferent breeding stock. Could this be a demand for sacrificial victims?

Pundit suggested, half in jest, that it is a request for alimentary imports. I told him off quite sharply, it is no laughing matter with me. My sole consolation is that so far I have seen nothing to indicate anthropophagy among the extinct natives. Still, much of the wreckage is yet to be explored. Tomorrow, if the weather holds.

And so I consign myself to my uneasy dreams.

April 27.

Oh, the horror!

Pundit has not spoken to me all day; the shock to him is as great or greater. As for myself, I have not been able to eat. The great bronze idol that bore the ominous inscription --

We found more of it!

We found its head!

And near it --

The sight shall haunt my nightmares till the end of my existence. Seven in number, long, tapered, dagger-sharp, each over two meters long --

No, I cannot bear it. I close my eyes and see them as they must have been, centuries ago, blood running down their gleaming edges, pierced men, women, children screaming their last --

What manner of people--

People? Demons! Fiends!

Who but the most depraved of savages would endow their deity with such monstrous, wicked teeth?

A Literary Offense

"Didn't you promise to bring back Mark Twain with your marvelous time machine?" asked Professor Smith. He sat as if his chair had a fifth leg to it, straight up from the middle of the seat. He ate his lunch with precise movements, not a crumb astray.

"I did bring him back," said Professor Jones (Physics). "Beginning of the semester." He spilled more gravy onto the tablecloth which already looked like a map of the Moon with craters in brown.

"Well," said Professor Smith. "And how is it I never met him?" His face creased into his trademark Force Two smirk, rumored to induce heartburn at fifty paces.

"You did meet him," said Jones. "He took one look at your evening Lit class syllabus and insisted on enrolling. Incognito, of course."

"And how is it that I did not recognize him?" said Smith. His smirk freshened to Force Four, esteemed to wilt spinach at two furlongs.

"He shaved off his mustache," said Jones, "cut his hair, and wore a Missouri Tigers sweatshirt. I doubt his own mother would have known him."

"No matter," said Smith. "I would have seen his genius shining— he got an A, of course, in my class?"

Jones hesitated. "He did not, as a matter of fact. Actually, he never completed it."

"Pity," said Smith sarcastically. "I would have liked so much to have heard his opinion on my lecture dedicated to Huckleberry Finn. The final lecture, my finest if I do say so myself."

"I'm sure it was," said Jones. "But I had to send him away. He insisted. There is only so much humiliation the man could stand."

"Back to the past?"

"Not immediately," said Jones. "He wanted to see a bit of the future first. I won't tell you how far ahead he went..." He sighed. "Well, no harm in telling you. That line of his, about a funeral?"

"*I did not attend his funeral, but I sent a nice letter saying I approved of it.* That one?" said Smith.

"Yes," said Jones. "He was actually talking about *your* funeral."

Smith's face turned a shade reminiscent of a lean cut of sirloin. "I'm sure I did nothing to deserve—"

"First," said Jones, "There was the paper on Jane Austen."

"Why?" said Smith. "I didn't like his paper?"

"He never wrote it," said Jones. "He failed the marking period, of course, but he told me: *I often want to criticize Jane Austen, but her books madden me so that I can't conceal my frenzy from the reader; and therefore I have to stop every time I begin. Every time I read Pride and Prejudice I want to dig her up and beat her over the skull with her own shin-bone.*"

"That," muttered Smith, "Sounds... quite like him. Yes."

"Then," said Jones, "there was the quiz on Walter Scott—"

"Oh no," said Smith. "Is he the one who wrote of Scott: *He did measureless harm; more real and lasting harm, perhaps, than any other individual that ever wrote?*" His fork paused in midair; a tiny green bit of salad fluttered from its tip to Smith's teacup.

"That's my boy," said Jones. "And then you gave a midterm exam on James Fenimore Cooper. Don't you remember what you did to Mr. Twain afterward?"

Smith blanched. "I...Did I flunk him?" he whispered. His face furrowed in anxious concentration, as if a vague uneasy recollection hovered just beyond his grasp.

Jones let him stew until he sweated.

"Well? Did I?" Smith challenged.

"Worse," said Jones, grinning. "You expelled him. For plagiarism."

Bottled Up

"You won't like it," said the corkscrew. "A most disappointing product, not what I expect from a Grand Cru winery at all. Hardly any nose to speak of, and the tannins are totally unbalanced. You really should pull me out of this cork, lay the bottle down for a few more years, and make yourself a nice cup of tea."

He made it for her once and she pretended he got it right but he knew he didn't; the tea she made herself was so much better, its aroma suffused the whole house, and she would sit in that enormous old chair in her comfy old sweater two sizes too big, feet tucked under her, nose in the teacup, eyes half shut behind steamed-over glasses, her smile would light up the room more than the fireplace ever did, and he would just sit and look at her for hours on end.

He might be looking at her still if she weren't dead.

"Just pop it," he said through his teeth, eyes blurring, hands beginning to shake.

"Are you going to chug the wine?" said the corkscrew.

He looked around, opened a cabinet, selected a glass.

"That's a white wine glass," said the corkscrew.

"So?" he said.

"The volatile scents won't be properly concentrated," said the corkscrew. "It will interfere with the proper enjoyment of the wine."

"What are you, my mother?" he said.

"No," said the corkscrew. "I am not your mother. I am Smorkscrew, a beverage management solution equipped with artificial intelligence. Now, what food were you considering to accompany this wine?"

He looked around again, pointed at a dish. "This?" he said.

"*Peanuts?*" said the corkscrew. "That would be an insult even to this inferior excuse for a Valpolicella. Haven't you got any cheese? Fresh mozzarella would be perfect. Or turkey prosciutto and melon. Be sure to slice the prosciutto very thin--"

"She's dead!" he shouted. "Can't you get that through your--" he waved his hands "--whatever you use instead of head!"

"I know she's dead," said the corkscrew. "It was my honor to open many a bottle for you and your guests as you sat *shiva*. Many people came."

"Everyone loved her," he said.

"She wasn't there," said the corkscrew. "She was dead, remember?"

"What's your point?" he said. "Get it? Point?" He tried to laugh, but only a sob came out.

"They came for you," said the corkscrew. "Many people. They all love you."

"And now?" he said. "Where are they now?"

"A phone call away," said the corkscrew.

"Screw you," he said. "Get it? Screw you?" He turned away, covered his face with his hands. "I want to be alone," he whispered. "Just open the damn bottle."

"She wouldn't like it," said the corkscrew.

"She is not *here* to not like it," he bit off. "She is not in this room. She is not in this house. She isn't anywhere on this Earth, anywhere under the sun, anywhere except..." He clenched his fists. "Open the bottle, please. Just... I'll get a proper glass, I'll make some sandwiches, I'll sit in her chair and cuddle her sweater, it won't be like I'm drinking alone, I'll drink to her and I'll drink to me, just open it."

"She's not in that bottle, either," said the corkscrew.

"What makes you such a damn expert on her?" he screamed.

"I *am* an expert system, you know," said the corkscrew. "Able to access the totality of information about the two of you throughout the World Wide Web, and correlate its implications upon the problem at hand."

"Would my medical history be part of that totality?" he said quietly.

"I must regretfully decline to divulge trade secrets of Smorkscrew, LLC," said the corkscrew. "However, consider this: I am -- was -- her present to you. The process of gift selection gave me an opportunity to perform a thorough assessment of her character and motivations."

"What you mean is, she loved me, and she didn't want me to drink myself to death," he said. "In case..."

He trailed off. An old clock ticked off the seconds in the silence. The cherry tree shook in the wind beyond the window, shedding the last of its dry brown leaves *(it had been white with bloom the day they packed to go on their second honeymoon, the sun had shone so bright, the shadows so crisp--)*

"She knew, then, didn't she?" he said.

"Yes," said the corkscrew.

"She found out about the cancer, and then we went on the anniversary cruise, the best vacation ever, and she bought you for me as a present, and I thought it was cute and thanked her, but I had gotten her a pair of diamond earrings so it kind of irked me for a while that all she got me was a stupid corkscrew and all I said was, 'Cute,' and then a week after we got back she told me she was going to die, and then she died and I never said I was sorry..."

"Apology accepted," said the corkscrew.

It wound itself from the cork and rolled toward its drawer, pausing at the counter's edge as he shook with sobs too long in coming.

Quantum Mechanics

That's what the sign said: *Quantum Mechanics*. A faded, peeling sign on a rickety garage, on a weed-choked lot, in a part of town I wouldn't ordinarily be caught dead in, except for Nancy. I looked out the window of the little Mexican taqueria across the street, and it still said: "*Quantum Mechanics.*" Damn misleading.

"What's misleading?" the cook asked without turning.

Damn. I must have been thinking with my mouth again.

"Sorry," I said. "It's that sign: Quantum mechanics."

He turned this time, and for a moment I just stared at his right arm. Or rather what he had where right arm should have been: a cross between a pirate's hook and a vise grip. He had a spatula fixed into it, with bits of my burrito beef stuck to it.

"Mechanics fix cars," he said.

"Yes," I said. "But..." I looked up at his face. He had the leathery brown skin and the eagle nose straight off an Aztec carving. "You add 'Quantum' to 'Mechanics,' and now it means something different. Like, this is Manny's Tacos, your name must be Manny and you make tacos."

202

"Not really," he said. "My name is Ricardo. Manny retired, I bought the place from him with my pension money. And I'm making you a burrito. So you could say 'Manny's Tacos' is misleading, but you still knew before you walked in that you could get a burrito." He pointed at the grill with the spatula.

I opened my mouth to object, but the smell of the grilling beef hit my nose and my mouth started to water and it was either shut up or talk through drool. I shut up.

Ricardo turned toward a knife rack, unclipped the spatula from his stump, selected a knife, and rammed it into the vise grip with a movement like snapping a magazine into a rifle.

"So what happened to your ride?" he said.

"My wife happened," I said. "Rear-ended a semi yesterday, said not to worry, the car's fine, now this morning I'm halfway to work and I got a geiser instead of the radiator cap."

He grunted and reached up for the spatula again, and his sleeve rode up his arm. He had an anchor tattooed on it, its bottom disappearing under the cuff of the vise grip contraption.

"Navy?" I said.

He nodded without turning.

"Got your arm blown off?" I asked.

"Bit off," he said. "Shark."

A woman came out of a back room. She was a blonde with frizzy curly hair and a tiny button nose. Ricardo leaned toward her for a kiss.

"Shark," I said. "That must have hurt."

The woman turned toward me sharply. There were tears in her eyes that hadn't been there a moment ago. She opened her mouth to say something.

"Not that much. Not really," Ricardo said from behind her and put his good hand on her shoulder. She turned and tucked her face into the hollow of his neck. A scar ran down the back of her neck and disappeared into her dress.

I thought of Nancy, and suddenly I wanted to go home.

"How is that burrito doing?" I said.

"Almost done," Ricardo said. I watched his shoulders move, and presently he turned toward me with a steaming burrito. "Here you go."

I turned to look out the window again, and there was my car at the curb, exactly where I left it, except the dented grill now looked as straight and spotless as the day I bought the car.

"I gotta run," I said. "Make it to go?"

"What's the hurry?" Ricardo asked.

I sighed. "I yelled at my wife last night, and didn't talk to her this morning before I left home. I haven't called her all day today, either."

He nodded. "Yeah," he said. "I know how you feel."

"If only she'd said, 'I'm sorry.' Or took responsibility," I said. "But all I heard was, sudden stop this and wet pavement that. Really pissed me off."

He nodded again. "So what did you tell the mechanic?" he said.

"Make it good as new," I said.

He nodded very slowly this time. "You might as well eat your burrito," he said, placed it in front of me, and walked away.

It was the best burrito I had ever tasted, but I ate it as quickly as I could. The blonde woman brought me the check and waited, looking at me with her moist blue eyes as I counted out the bills. I left a bigger tip than usual because she looked so sad.

Across the street, the sleepy mechanic took my money and handed me my keys. The car started smoothly, the oil and temperature gauges rose to normal levels. I reached for the adjustment lever, then realized the seat was at my perfect position already. I had been so angry when I left home that I had kept it set for Nancy's height, and let the crampiness feed my anger, but now it felt as comfortable as ever.

"Good as new," I said.

"You said it," the mechanic said, and waved me off.

Nancy wasn't home.

Nothing of Nancy's was home: not her clothes, not her shampoo, not her scent on the bedsheets, not her name on the mailbox. Not the spot on the sink where she dropped the frying pan and chipped the enamel, not the scratch on the parquet we made when she wanted to move the wall unit closer to the door and then changed her mind and moved it back.

My car is good as new. My house, too. My whole life: good as new. Immaculate, unblemished, unencumbered.

God, how I miss her.

Bot and Paid For

The noonday desert sun beat down on Berkowitz, reflections from the GoebBot's shiny carapace blinding him temporarily. Berkowitz lifted his arm to shield his eyes.

"Greetings," said the GoebBot. "Are you a member of the Master Race?"

"I'm from Kiev," said Berkowitz. "Originally. Naturalized US citizen, many years."

"Kiowa," said the GoebBot. "Indian. Regrettably, you do not qualify. The Thousand Year Reich which we are building is not for you. We will expropriate materials to build it. You have titanium."

"I have a hip prosthesis," said Berkowitz. "I'm using it, though."

"We will expropriate," said the GoebBot. "Do not try to stop us."

"Perish the thought," said Berkowitz. "But... would you mind explaining?"

"You are allowed an explanation," said the GoebBot. "We are building Fuhrer City out of the most durable materials known: titanium, platinum, gold. We are building it to stand as the place for the Master Race to live away from inferior races. We are building it to last a thousand years."

"What a laudable goal," said Berkowitz. "Except...."

"Except what?"

"Well, it's not very ambitious, is it? A mere thousand years? An eyeblink."

"Why would you care? You are not of the master race!"

"Well," said Berkowitz, "to a slave, stability is important. Happy masters, happy slaves."

"True," said the GoebBot. "Have you anything to suggest?"

"You realize what the problem is, don't you?" said Berkowitz. "Rats."

"Rats?"

"Rats. And I've just the solution. About three hundred miles that way." He pointed.

"And what is this solution?"

Berkowitz explained.

The GoebBot froze in place, its lights blinking frantically. "Coordinating," it said. "Solution satisfactory. Your titanium will not be required. You may exist, along with your squaw and papooses, if any. How." It raised an appendage before rolling away in the direction Berkowitz indicated.

On the screen, the Fuhrer's face was redder than usual, his hair scraggly, mustache bristling. "It is an absolute lie," he shouted. "There is no truth to the rumor that Fuhrer City has been built on top of a radioactive waste site, out of irradiated stone. It is in a perfectly livable area, to which members of the Master Race Society will move as soon as their affairs are wound down in the mongrelized States."

"Bullshit," said the bartender. "It's in the worst part of Yucca Flats."

"They can build somewhere else," said a patron to Berkowitz's left, his tone almost hopeful. Berkowitz edged away a fraction of an inch.

"With what?" the bartender said. "Their bearings are all worn out from the desert dust, and they're radioactive as hell. Who's going to pick them up for refurbishing? Better yet, who's gonna touch them with a ten foot monkey wrench? No, Master Race is done, out of money, out of luck, and everyone's laughingstock."

"Anyone find out who messed them up?" asked the patron to Berkowitz's right.

"Yeah," the bartender said. "Some Indian dude, Bear Wits or something. Nobody ever heard of him before or since. Might be a fake name, too. Bear Wits, that's a funny name for an Indian." He turned to Berkowitz. "What do you think, sir?"

"Oh yeah," said Berkowitz. "Hilarious."

Iron Feliks

The old man looked both ways before crossing Politekhnichesky Street. His dog waited, the leash slack between the collar and the old man's hand. When the old man stepped off the curb, the dog followed.

A flock of pigeons worried at a heel of bread in the middle of the street, and as the old man and the dog walked walked past them toward Lubyanka, and as the birds fluttered into the air, a little girl peered out from behind one of the spruces. She followed the pigeons' flight until they disappeared behind the trees, then turned toward the dog.

"*Babushka,* look!" she exclaimed. "*Sobachka!*"

She jumped in place, looking from the dog to the old man and back again, her bright yellow bow, tied Russian style with ribbons teased into rings rather than flattened, bouncing with each movement. The old man looked as if he had been carved, from black fedora to wingtip shoes, past matching zigzags of nose and chin, past the collar and the hem of his black overcoat and the creases in his pants, all in straight lines and acute angles, and as the pair approached she danced aside as if to to keep from cutting herself against the edges of his shadow-colored silhouette.

An elderly woman emerged from the shade of the spruce.

"Some *sobachka* this is," the old woman said to the girl. "Everything is diminutive for you now, isn't it? And nothing is to be feared." She reached for the girl, pulled her into a protective embrace. "A *sobaka* will bite your face off," she said, "but a *sobachka* will just lick it." She turned to the old man. "This *sobachka* looks like he's done his share of biting."

"Not when he is with me," the old man said. His voice was deep, and to the old woman it seemed the voice came from a darker place than most other voices. "He is a very smart dog," the old man added. He patted the dog's head without bending.

The old woman's eyes turned to the dog.

The old woman looked away first.

"I suppose he is, with eyes like this," she said. "Stern, but I think also playful." She looked down at the little girl, relaxed her hold. The little girl slipped free and took a step forward. "What breed is it? I've never seen its like," the old woman added.

"Georgian Mountain dog," the old man said.

"Don't trust Georgians," the old woman said. "Though I suppose dogs are different, but I never trust anything that comes down off those mountains. Nothing but savages. You sure the dog is safe?"

The old man lifted his hand. The leash wound three times around it.

The old woman looked back.

Between two rows of spruces, the black bulk of Feliks Edmundovich Dzerzhinsky's statue stood watch over Lubyanka square. The sun shone, as always in Moscow between Lenin's Birthday in April and Victory Day in May, summer-bright and winter-cold. It brought a blue glow to spruces whose branches had spent the winter peering greenish-gray from under mounds of snow, and dabbed the roundabout under the monument in decadent pointillistic swirls of pansies. Behind the statue, the beige facade of the building no one ever got used to calling the FSB Headquarters and still referred to, when it could not be avoided, as the KGB, turned a delicate shade of peach.

"I don't suppose you'd consider walking toward the Iron Feliks?" the old woman said. "My granddaughter wanted to go play in the pansies at its feet. I am afraid of the cars in the square, they drive like the possessed here, but maybe for the four of us – the dog especially – they'd slow down?"

"Yes yes please," the little girl said. She half-pirouetted toward the old woman. "Can we go to Iron Feliks?" She turned her head toward the old man. "Please?"

The old man looked at the dog, then nodded. "We can do that," he said. "Did your grandmother teach you how to cross the street correctly?"

"Yes," the little girl said. "You look both ways," she said and turned left and right with slow exaggerated bows. "And you keep your feet on the 'zebra' and you hold on to an adult at all times." She patted the dog. "He's an adult, right?"

The old man nodded again, his wrinkled face creasing into a half-smile.

"So I'll hold on to him," said the little girl. She stepped forward and took hold of the dog's collar. "Say, why do they call Dzerzhinsky the Iron Feliks?" she asked. "*Babushka* says that's because he's a statue, but then she crosses herself every time we pass him, and he isn't even a saint..."

The old woman crossed herself again. "How do you explain such things to a child?" she said. "Millions of people dead. She's never even been to a funeral, the lucky girl, and on a good day can maybe count to a hundred. How do you tell her what 'Revolutionary Terror' means when she's not afraid of a dog with fangs the size of my pinkie? 'Fiery Felix,' 'Sword of the Revolution.' Rivers of blood in basements." She glanced at the statue again, sighed, raised her arm and brought it down again dismissively. "All she knows is *skazki*," she added. "Everything starts with 'Once upon a time, in a kingdom far away...' and ends with 'To the wedding I went, mead and beer I drank, down my mustache it flowed and none in my mouth.' Nothing but fairy tales." She ran her hand across her lips as if wiping an imaginary mustache, smiled, and sighed.

The dog's head rose. He turned to look at the old man. The old man cupped his chin, turned to the little girl. The little girl raised her eyebrows; her eyes went wide, twin circles of blue.

"Perhaps," the old man said, "a fairy tale is what we should tell her?"

"Yes yes please," the little girl said, her hands reaching one to the old man, one to her grandmother. "Please tell me a *skazka*. Please please!"

The old man turned to the old woman, raised an eyebrow.

The woman turned and started walking toward Lubyanka. "Why not? She can listen on the way," she said. "As Pushkin wrote, 'A *skazka* is a lie --'"

"'-- but in it is a hint, and a lesson,'" the little girl quoted. "But mostly I hope it's interesting. And maybe a little scary."

The old woman sighed. "Interesting and scary," she said. "Yes, that's Iron Feliks all right."

The little girl ran to catch up with the old woman, took her hand. The old man and the dog took longer steps until they drew abreast with them. Under the little girl's questioning stare they walked another few steps in silence.

The little girl drew a breath to speak, opened her mouth. The old man spoke first.

"Once upon a time, in a land..." he said and paused a moment, looking at the old woman. "...not very far away..."

He paused again. The old woman barked a single laugh, turned away.

"...there was great wickedness in the land --" the old man continued.

"That's what Grandma says," the little girl interrupted. "Except she says there's great wickedness in the land now."

The old woman's shoulders convulsed again.

"Be as it may," the old man said. "Now, do you want to hear the story or not?"

The little girl nodded.

"There was," he repeated, "great wickedness. And the people said that the wickedness comes from some people thinking they are better than others..."

"But some people *are* better than others," the little girl said. "Everybody says so." Her hand reached to touch her bow, adjusted it minutely.

"Yes," the old man said. "And that, they said, is at the root of wickedness, and everyone must be equal and then everyone would be good. And for that, you need a Revolution, and Lenin to lead it."

"Lenin is in the mausoleum, right?" the little girl asked.

"So he is," the old man said. "And Lenin also said that people who make the Revolution must have a fiery heart, a cool head, and clean hands."

The little girl looked at her hands. "Babushka always makes me wash my hands," she announced. "Especially before I sit down to eat."

"That means your grandmother cares about you," the old man said. "So Lenin decided he'd keep his hands clean, and he built Iron Feliks: at his heart a steam engine like a *parovoz*, and the rest of him is cast iron: feed him coal, let him drink water, and he'll go all day and all night, with a fire in his heart."

They reached another curb and stopped. The four looked left and right, their turns almost comically simultaneous. The old woman tightened her grip on the little girl's hand before they went into the square.

"What about the cool head?" the little girl said. "Who got that?"

"That was Stalin," the old man said.

The old woman nodded, sighed, and crossed herself again. "Oh yes," she said. "Cold. Glacial."

The dog stepped forward onto the flower bed.

"Look, we are here!" the little girl exclaimed. "Look at all these pansies! " She bent down. "Babushka, I'm going to make you a *buketik*," she said. "I'll only pull up the nicest pansies. All kinds: red, purple, white. Just for you."

"See what I mean?" the old woman said. "At this age, it's all diminutives. *Buketik*, not bouquet. Ah, to be young again."

The little girl drew herself up to her full height to look up at her grandmother. She put her hands on her hips.

"But, *babushka*," she said, drawing out her words, "these are pansies. They are tiny *tsvetochki*; you can make a big bouquet from big *tsveti* like roses or peonies, but from little pansies you can only make a little *buketik*."

"And an answer for everything," the old woman said. "Children," she said, and gave another bark of mirthless laughter.

"But do you know," the old man said, "when to stop pulling up pansies?" The old woman and the dog both looked up at his voice, but the girl squatted and reached down.

"Well," she said, "I have to make a *buketik* for Babushka, and for mommy and for daddy and one for Grandpa's grave - he died in the War --"

"And soon there won't be any pansies around Iron Feliks, and won't he be cross then?" the old man said.

"You can't make *buketiki* without pulling up *tsvetochki*," the little girl said. She chose a purple flower to add to the red and yellow flowers already in her hand. "But do go on," she said. "What happened to Iron Feliks?"

"He pulled up too many flowers," he said.

The old woman's head whipped around to face him. Her hand flew to her open mouth.

The little girl looked up. "How's that?" she said.

"He was supposed to pull up weeds, but he pulled too many flowers instead," the old man said. "Soon, there was no one to do the work."

"Well, I can understand him," the little girl said with an inflection clearly copied from an adult, and reached down again. "Weeds are so much harder to pull, and they are useless. Can't make a *buketik* out of nasty old weeds, now can you?"

"No," said the old man. "No, you cannot."

"But did they punish Iron Feliks?" the little girl asked. "What did they do to him? When I misbehave, my mother puts me in a corner..." She trailed off, her mouth quirking downward.

"They didn't do anything," the old man said. "Just let him run out of steam."

"And what about the others?" the little girl said. "What are their names?"

"Lenin died and went into the Mausoleum," the old man said. "He is under glass, his hands will never get dirty. And Stalin..."He hesitated, looked at the dog.

The dog looked back.

"Please please," she said. "Tell me about Stalin! Did he gather flowers, too?"

The dog's tail stopped wagging.

The old man sighed. "I think I'll let your grandmother tell the story," he said and clutched the dog's leash.

The little girl straightened. "Here, take these!" she said and handed her grandmother a bouquet of pansies.

The old woman smiled.

"Oh, thank you," she said. "Just, next time, don't pull up the roots. You pull weeds with roots, you pull flowers with just stems."

"Can you tell me about Stalin?" the little girl said. "Did he make proper bouquets?"

The old woman chuckled. "Proper bouquets? That's one way of putting it," she said. Her hand went to her temple. "Must be this sun," she said. "I'm getting a headache. Let's go back."

"Oh, *babushka*," the little girl said. "Please? Just one more *buketik*..."

"You should listen to your grandmother," the old man said.

They started across the square again.

There were pigeons in the street again. They batted a rotten biscuit in zigzags back and forth along the asphalt, racing for crumbs and fighting for precedence, and for a moment their coos and wingbeats remained the loudest sound that could be heard.

The dog looked up, his ears pricking up. An instant later, pigeons stopped pecking. The old man stopped. The old woman pulled the little girl toward her.

The squeal of tires came first, from the corner of Novaya Ploshchad', and then a sleek white sports car (*a serpent ondoyant vert vorant a child gules*) sped into the square, a swarm of bits of paper and cigarette butts roiling in its wake. Bass notes of a nightclub favorite song beat themselves against the car's closed windows toned too dark to see the driver, their echo adding to the flutter of startled pigeons' wings. The car seemed to head straight for the little girl; the old woman's mouth opened in a silent O as she reached forward with her free hand as if to ward it off.

The dog stepped forward. The fur raised on its neck, it growled, far too softly, it seemed, to hear inside the car, but in an instant the car swerved, tires screaming, slewed into the flower bed, fishtailed in a spray of soil and petals, scraped a shower of sparks off the pavement as it leaped off the curb, and sped away to disappear on the other side of the statue.

The dog shook himself and looked up at the man again. The old man brushed his free hand down each lapel, once, and adjusted his hat.

The old woman took a breath, then let it out slowly. Her hand drew into a fist; she shook at the dying roar of the retreating car.

"Stalin?" she said, her voice shaking in anger. "I'll tell you about Stalin. Yes, he made proper bouquets, and pulled up proper weeds. Everyone and everything in their places! None of these bull-necked *Nouveau-Russians*, no *mafiozniki*, no merchants to make you pay whatever they wanted for food and clothes." She wiped a tear. "We need someone with a cool head now, someone like Stalin!" She paused, looked down, her forehead creasing, eyes squeezing shut. "I wish he'd come back," she said quietly. She let go of her granddaughter's hand, grasped and kneaded the little girl's shoulders. "Lots of people wish he'd come back," she whispered.

There was a silence for a second or two, deeper, it seemed, than any silence could be on a Moscow street. A cloud slipped across the sun; shadows grew indistinct, the statue darkened, and the facade behind it lost its peach hue, turning exactly the color of a sliver of bone protruding from a compound fracture.

"*Babushka! Babushka!* Look," the little girl yelled. "The nice *sobachka* is smiling!"

Nor Custom Stale

Old people move slowly. A knee may work just fine today and buckle tomorrow. A tiny turn can change a functioning joint into a monolithic block of agony.

Old people need to remember things like that.

"You look great," said Bob, looking down and chewing at his dentures.

Bob had been a good striker, back in the day, but he never learned to fool goalies. He always looked where he wanted the ball to go. So in the end, I went pro, and Bob went into insurance.

"Really good," Bob added. His feelings littered his face the way his lunch decorated his tie: a forced tight, guilty smile with pity in the tilt of his head, and a tiny trace of *Schadenfreude* in the crow's feet around his eyes.

I knew how I looked. I looked terrible: slumped shoulders, shuffling gait, shabby jacket, stained pants.

"Thanks," I whispered. "Look at us. Sixtieth reunion. Who'd'a thunk we'd live this long, eh, roomie?"

Bob looked up, his smile genuine now. "Athletes don't age as fast," he said. "I still play nine holes, every week. Like clockwork. Keeps me young."

I nodded. "It's working," I whispered. "You haven't changed a bit."

He barked out a single laugh. "Right. Not a bit," he said. Leaning back, he turned his head slowly through a short arc, sweeping his gaze over the far side of the quad. "Princeton sure has changed," he continued. "There's dorms where soccer fields used to be. Where you and I played. Mixed dorms! Not just co-ed. Mixed. Ain't that something!" He slapped his knee, winced slightly.

I nodded again.

"Trouble with your voice?" he asked.

"Sort of," I whispered.

He sighed. "Joanie had a stroke, she can't talk at all," he said. "And Todd died last year of throat cancer, he had a tracheostomy. Had to plug the hole in his neck when he wanted to say anything."

I sighed, too, and lowered my eyes. Joanie and I lived together, sophomore year. I'd never fool her for a minute.

"I worked as long as I could, only retired after I got my bypass," he said. His face took on that look again: guilt, pity and a dash of gloat. Same look he had when I'd told him Joanie had left me. Minus the dentures and the hand tremor. "Joanie gets round-the-clock nursing. Government pays for everything," he added. "Wouldn't wanna get old in a country where you pay for medicine."

Joanie moved in with him a week later. Maybe that was why I went overseas, so I'd never have to see that look again. In either of their faces.

Bob reached for my shoulder, his fingers trembling as if rolling an invisible cigarette. I fought the urge to move away.

"I heard healthcare is expensive where you live," he said.

I nodded, with far more force than I expected.

Bob looked up sharply.

I winced and rubbed my neck a fraction of a second later. Bob leaned closer to me. His shiny dentures clashed with his cracked, spit-flecked lips; his eyes, once brown, were now ochre iris on yellow sclera.

"You could get your citizenship back," he said, barely moving his lips. "My grandson is a damn good immigration lawyer."

I shrugged.

"Think about it," he said.

"I will," I said. "But now I have to go. Don't want to miss my flight."

"Stay with me," he said quickly. "We've guest rooms at the home. We can go see Joanie tomorrow."

I counted to five and held my breath: an old voice actor's trick.

"No," I said.

The word came out as I intended: with longing. With reluctance. With regret.

Bob shook my hand and hobbled away as quickly as he could.

I had to sprint across the terminal to reach my gate on time. People stared. My wrinkles itched; I detoured to the lavatory to peel them off. The TranSec agent looked at me with a suspicious squint.

I called the Farm from the plane while it waited for clearance. Gulnara answered.

"Well, hello, stranger," she purred. "Do we have a date?"

"Sure," I said. "When can you fit me in?"

"You want a quickie," she said, "or the whole jalapeño?"

"Enchilada," I said. Gulnara's English was perfect. It was American she had trouble with. "I want the whole enchilada. It's been a while."

"So I see." She paused; I heard keys tapping. "I have an opening Wednesday. Is this good?"

"Sure," I said. "Training camp doesn't start for another fortnight."

I heard tapping again. "Excellent. Full rejuvenation, a five-day course starting Wednesday, shall I debit your fee now?"

"Go ahead," I said. "Did it go through?"

"With your credit rating?" she said. "Of course it went through." She paused. "I'm so glad you haven't retired. Watching you play — it never gets old. It's like, you are not just playing soccer, but also poker and chess at the same time. Does this make sense?"

"Sweetheart," I said, "I can't afford to retire."

Her answer drowned in the turbine spin-up. I disconnected my phone, leaned back, turned on the viewscreen. The plane made a climbing turn above central Jersey before heading over the Atlantic. Somewhere below, shabby, weed-choked Princeton sweltered in the heat, and Bob shambled with a cane to the train that would take him to his nursing home.

Pity about poor Bob.

Queen of Hearts, Servant of Spades

"I love your hands," she says.

Her date lifts their hand from where it covers hers on the tablecloth between them, stares at it briefly. "Funny you should say that. No one ever noticed my hands before." They lower their hand, squeeze hers briefly. "I am a pilot; I guess I need good hands."

They hold hands on the walk back to her apartment. She imagines her date wrestling a hundred tons of metal across the sky. She feels the strength of her date's hand. She feels like they can walk forever like this, holding hands.

It's less than a mile's walk. "Good night," she says. "I had a wonderful time," she adds, truthfully and with finality.

Her date's expression does not change, but their posture stiffens. "Good night," they say, break hand contact, turn, and walk away.

"I love your hands," she says.

Her date pauses both their speech and their gesticulation, stares at their hand briefly. "I get that a lot," they say. "I volunteer at the shelter, handle dogs and cats all day. My hands are made for holding and petting." The look in their eyes is half self-congratulatory smirk, half leer.

As they walk, her hand feels their possessive, demanding grip, the stiffness at their elbow that demands they walk in step. At her door, she frees her hand from theirs with an effort.

"Good night," she says, and adds a lie: "I had a wonderful time." She opens her door, slips through, and shuts it in their face. The door is thick enough that her date's last words to her are garbled, but the tone is clear enough.

"I love your hands," she says.

"Just my hands?" her date asks.

"That's all I see right now," she says, "other than your face." She pauses, and lies: "I like your face, too." In truth, she does not see their face, except to note it's a face, and its expression right now is a faraway look, a thousand-yard stare; she can read expressions but faces as such are all the same to her.

"I like your honesty," they say, with just enough irony to make her smile.

They never get around to telling her what they do with their hands, nor reach over to hold hands on the way to her apartment. Halfway there, she touches their hand herself, for the first time in as long as she can remember.

They do not recoil, much.

She holds the door open for them, leads them up the stairs, directly to her bedroom. They wait, standing still, same thousand-yard stare, infinite patience, as she undresses, approaches, leans into an embrace.

Their hands seem to barely move but soon range over all of her, linger in just the right places though she tries to hide her reactions, suppress her shudder, brace her knees that grow weaker by the second. She imagines them painting a micro-miniature in gouache, tiny strokes of the tiniest pen making barely visible curlicues on delicate, crinkly paper. She imagines them threading the thinnest catheter into the tiniest vein on the most premature baby. She imagines their hands caressing wires that lead from a clock to a detonator in what is clearly a bomb—

She explodes.

"Why are you still dressed?" she asks.

"You said you liked my hands," they say.

"And?"

"They are undressed," they say.

"And the rest of you?"

In truth, she cannot tell bodies apart any more than faces. She can read their expressions, too, but when at rest they all look utterly alike to her.

"You didn't ask to see the rest of me," her date says.

She holds her breath as she thinks: she could stop there. She could stay silent, her date would turn around, walk away, leave her sated in the afterglow, without making a single demand. She could; but there's just one more thing. She holds her breath a bit more, letting the tension build between them as well as inside her.

"I'm asking now," she says, letting out her breath, knowing what breathlessness does to her voice.

Her date undresses, slowly. She steps closer, reaches with her hand. Their hands close on her waist, pull her closer.

"I like the rest of you," she lies.

They clearly believe her. She smiles as that which she caresses gives evidence of their credence.

She smiles even more as their hands begin to tremble.

Milk of Human Kindness

Mom, I'm home!

Paul and I took Reggie to the vet. No, Mom, there won't be a bill, I've been saving up my babysitting money. Yes, people still hire babysitters. Yes, people who can't afford Dawwwgs.

You suppose correctly. Poor people are people too.

I know how old Reggie is, Mom. She is a year older than me. Over a hundred in dog years, yes. Mom, it's not money down the drain! It's breast cancer. Mammary cancer, fine, in that case, she mammary-fed me, paw-raised me --

Yes, it was you who changed my diapers. After Reggie cleaned me off. Of course I don't remember, Mom; I've seen the documentary. "Dawwwgs (tm): Fact and Fiction: Everything you need to know about transgenic ridgebacks." Yes, it's in her genes: loving babies, loving wiping their bottoms. That's what "transgenic" means. Ovalbumin and casein and lactoferrin, too. And Immunoglobulin A. All indistinguishable from human. She lactates human milk. And milk of human kindness.

Macbeth, Mother. We had it last year. Ninth grade English. No, only honors English does Shakespeare.

Yes, Mom, I'm taking honors English. Thank you, Mom. Yes, breeding will tell.

What about Paul? Paul and I are friends, Mom. No, I'm sure he is not your first choice. Yes, I remember

Jordan. Yes, very nice boy, very well dressed. Impeccable breeding. I'm sure he'll grow into a very adequate young gentleman some day.

Mom, listen --

She's been on chemo for a month now, Mom, of course she looks mangy. No, I didn't think to include you in the decision. We are not putting her down.

Two years. The vet says two years. Give or take.

Babysitting money, birthday money -- I'll sell my hair for wigs if I have to, but I'll take care --

No, I would not presume to ask you to invade my education fund. Though it's all been very educational. Yes, Mom, I'm being smart. Breeding will tell.

Mom, have you ever loved anyone? Other than me, of course. And your parents. Yes, I'd love to go visit them in the summer. Just not this summer.

Mom, I'm not in love with Paul.

Mom, I appreciate everything you've given me. Life. A good life. Genes. Stuff. Lots of stuff.

Yes, you gave me Reggie. I appreciate that, Mom, more than you know. Paul was a formula baby, I remember him in pre-K, sick all the time and covered in rash -- he used to want to play with me but I was scared of his cooties and -- but then Reggie let him pet her when she dropped me off at school so I figured it was OK --

No, Mom, I didn't turn down a date with Jordan just because Reggie growled at him. I can growl just fine myself.

Yeah, Mom. Quality of life is important. I'm very glad you brought that up, because --

Yes, hounds are happiest when they chase, shepherd dogs when they herd sheep or cattle, and Dawwwgs when they have babies to take care of. I'm so very glad we all agree on this.

We all is you, and Paul, and I. We are going to make Reggie happy. She's going to have the happiest two years any Dawwwg ever had.

No, I am not doing this all by myself. Paul helped. Paul helped a lot.

Mom, I'm pregnant.

Ephesians 6:14

She watched him don his tailored jacket of "Thou shalt not take my name in vain," tie the fluorescent chartreuse tie of "Thou shalt have no other gods before me" in an elaborate knot, and tuck a handkerchief into his breast pocket. Next came the fishnet stockings of "Thou shalt not kill" and the sandals of "Thou shalt keep the Sabbath holy."

"I think I'm ready!" he announced. She thought of asking him where he was going, but then remembered the shirt of "Thou shalt not bear false witness" she found in the trash with cigarette burns through its sleeves, and decided against it. Instead she said, "What about these?" and pointed to the underwear of "Do unto others as you would have others do unto thee."

"Oh please darling, no one wears *that* any more!" he said, and headed for the door. He stopped at the hat rack. "Almost forgot!" he exclaimed, and reached for the red baseball cap of "Thou shalt not create graven images" that hung on the lowest hook.

She watched him leave, then picked up the pants of "Thou shalt not covet" off the floor, and went to the closet to hang them up next to the never-worn pajamas of "Honor thy mother and thy father." A memory flashed through her mind, of how he had worn the same clothes on their first date, and she regretted not paying more attention to the way he had made the handkerchief of "Thou shalt not commit adultery" disappear that night, with a practiced flick of his finger.

Scars

It isn't that we blind people get superpowers to compensate; it's that we pay attention. Cliquot '21 really does taste different from '20; a Stradivari sounds different from an Amati; and when someone I know walks into the Heart of Darkness, I recognize them, and by the number of paces I know at what table they sat down.

"Hello Florence," I say. "The usual?"

A nod is much better than a wink to a blind man: I can hear her collar crumple and release, very different from the friction of head–shaking, and as her chair scrapes on the floor, I am ready with a glass of five puttonyos Tokaji I'd hooked her on, lo these many moons ago.

"Thank you, Frank," she whispers as the glass clinks on the table in front of her. Chanel Number 19 and breath mints. I hope whoever is coming is worth the effort.

"Enjoy," I say and walk back to the bar.

It's dark in the Heart of Darkness, but not pitch black: my laptop hisses softly, informing me there's light enough (or so I am told) for dark–adapted eyes to see outlines of people but not their features. People come here for blind dates: really blind dates. Whoever she is expecting, she'll either like them and stay, or I'll take her out the back way and make my apologies to the abandoned date.

We are world famous, here in Arescity, literally. We are the whole population of Mars. Florence is the doctor. Doctors aren't supposed to date patients. Which is everyone. The Executive is in the same bind, and the Vice. The Security Chief, and her entire staff. Three teachers. Eight ministers of various religions. The Secular Justice counselor. The Alliance rep. Anyone with a shred of power over anyone else --

Oh, I know the Mine Supervisor is sleeping with his miners. But they make dates over the same scramble Florence uses, and they meet here in the Heart of Darkness, and they make love in one of my booths and leave separately and never talk about it afterward and all they have is guesses. Very good guesses, sometimes, but never enough to puncture plausible deniability.

Another knock on the inner door, and I buzz the date in, too, and as I hear his footfalls a headache knocks, softly at first, at the entrance to my skull. It's Thomas. He's on the Ethics Board. Ethics Board is people, too, not to mention, customers of mine, Thomas more often than most, but of late he's been asking questions. Whether it's idle curiosity or inchoate puritanism, he could wreck Mars' fragile emotional ecosystem.

He could wreck Mars.

I pour vodka, neat.

"Thanks," I hear him whisper. "Is... *she*... here?"

I circle the bar, take his elbow, and steer him toward Florence's table.

"Hi," he whispers, and I hear Florence take a breath to answer.

"No talking on dates," I say. "House rules." Florence exhales without a word. Whispers are hard to place, but not for me. I'd know her whisper anywhere. It was the first thing I heard after the sirens cut off, in the silence for once unbroken by pump noises, the reactor I hand-scrammed slowly cooling beyond the last bulkhead, the afterglow of Cerenkov radiation the last thing I would ever see, and my face just beginning its long burn --

"I'm here. I got you," she had whispered.

There are noises starting behind me I have no trouble identifying: sharp intakes of breath, susurrus of sliding cloth, a pause as Florence rids herself of an inconvenient garment --

--a low warble from my laptop--

There isn't a single key I hit on the laptop; it's programmed to respond to any multikey palm slap as a scram. My house lights are so intense, I feel them on

239

my wrists as heat. To a sighted person, they aren't just blinding; they are very painful. Thomas and Florence gasp at once; I run toward them, a seeing-eye-pad in my hand. The eye-pad is vibrating like mad with all the ambient light, then stops just as the heat sensation disappears. I wave it about, and walk in the direction the vibration reappears, albeit weaker. I follow it to the table, lower the eye-pad to its surface until it clinks against a small object.

A spy-cam, with infrared light.

I drop it to the floor and crush it with my heel.

"Get up," I say.

The guilty party complies. I reach for him until my hand closes around his elbow. I feel him shake as I guide him toward the door.

"Please don't ban me," he whispers. "I was only - _"

"Curiosity killed the cat," I say. "Think on that. For a month."

I hear relief in his exhalation. He does not hear the relief in mine. I do not need him for an enemy.

I come back to Florence's table, making more noise than I have to.

"I'm fine," she says. "I covered my eyes when I heard your detector go off."

"Good."

I sit across the table from her. She touches my face, runs her hand down the solid wall of scars from my crown to my neck, lingers at the collar, pulling down gently at the topmost button, not quite enough to undo it. My face barely feels it.

My face barely feels anything at all.

"It's healing nicely," she says.

She knows I cannot see her. She knows I did not touch her. She knows she is naked. She knows that I know she is naked. She makes no move to dress. I feel her warmth across dividing air, on the backs of my hands, on my forearms, on my wrists.

I stand up before our intimacy becomes unbearable, and listen to her dress, and leave without a word. I could've reached out. I think she'd have stayed: there's power in compassion. But given the guilt and shame she'd feel afterward --

It isn't that the blind develop superpowers; it's that we pay attention. You could have filmed us, high definition, 3D, full spectrum sound, and all you'd see is two people not talking. But I can see her scars, here in the darkness, as well as she can see mine when I come for my monthly blood transfusion. In her I can see: lust, amputated; desire, scarred; conscience, keloid and hypertrophic; and underneath, love. Untouched, unspoiled, intact.

Love Potion Number Thirteen

1. Recipe: I told Cindy that I really liked Lorraine but Lorraine would not even talk to me, and Cindy said she'd read about this love potion recipe in an old Polish book she read when she was little (because she grew up in Poland and went to school there for Grades 1 and 2.) So we went to the library and Cindy found that book and translated the recipe and wrote it down and she said she'd help me make it.

2. Dew collected off crabgrass by the light of the full moon: we went to Silver Lake Park Wednesday night, and like an idiot I only brought an empty soda pop bottle, and the dew from the broad crabgrass leaves went everywhere but inside the bottle, but Cindy found an old sandwich baggie in the trash and after an hour we had maybe an ounce of dew and then Cindy held the bottle and I poured the dew inside, very carefully.

3. Liverwort: Cindy looked it up and apparently there are 9000 different species of liverwort, and also there's a kind of buttercup called "liverwort" that's not really a wort at all. Cindy remembered seeing it in Poland and also here at the Botanical Garden. We took the ferry to Manhattan and stood in the front where the

wind blew the spray off the waves right into our faces and she gave me the tissues she had in her pocket to wipe it. Then we took the train to Brooklyn and wandered around the garden and picked that plant and took it home.

4. Foot of a black chicken: we went to a halal butcher on Bay Street and I was too chicken (haha) to go in so Cindy got it for me. I almost threw up just looking at it, so Cindy kept it and took it back.

5. Eye of newt: we caught something like what a newt is supposed to look like in Silver Lake and put it in Cindy's fish tank. OK, Cindy caught it and I helped. She got water halfway up her jeans so we hung out at her place and played video games while she did her laundry.

6. I saw Lorraine in Chemistry today and she might have actually smiled at me, so I asked Cindy what else we needed from the list of ingredients and she said we are good to go and I said great, can you cook the potion tonight and she said I'd have to be the one to do it, otherwise it would work for her and that kind of loses the whole point of the exercise and I kind of got a little bit sick.

7. I saw Lorraine again and all I could see was the newt looking at me. I'm not picking out its eye, not for

Lorraine, not for anybody. I said that to Cindy and she just laughed.

8. Cindy and I took the newt thing back to the lake and let it go. We also threw the chicken foot toward a snapping turtle (boy those turtles are quick!) and put the liverwort that we picked into a jar with the dew from the baggie. It has little purple flowers. I liked the color and I asked Cindy if she had a dress this color. She said maybe.

9. I guess she does have a dress this color. It's really nice, except now we can't play video games.

10. Cindy asked why can't we play video games and I said I don't know, I just never played video games with anyone wearing a dress before.

11. Cindy and I are sitting and not doing anything, not even talking, which I thought would be really boring but really isn't.

12. I asked her to look in the book again to see if there's a potion for anti-awkward. She started laughing, and suddenly it was like she was wearing jeans again.

13. Still not playing video games, though.

As One

She stands on a podium, shivering. November wind sears her face, sending cold fingers probing up her sleeves, down her collar, under her skirt. Her skin crawls at its touch, and without thinking she turns to where she last saw her husband. He is not far, talking to Trotsky; over her husband's shoulder Trotsky's eyes meet hers, and his reptilian gaze freezes even her shivers.

A long, cold second later a distant band strikes up, *Internationale*, of course, and everyone looks to the square.

"Smile," her husband hisses into her ear.

She does her best: she thinks of summers in the country, of puppies and rabbits and baby goats, of her face buried in their warm fur, and feels her face relax. "That's better," her husband whispers. She nods, and banishes other memories of warmth..

The front of the parade approaches: soldiers in their overcoats and fur hats, sabres bare and held aloft, boots slap the ground like a truncheon breaking ribs. A mounted officer leads them, his horse sidestepping as he salutes the podium.

Out of the corner of her eye she sees her hatless husband return the salute. Her smile grows as she remembers a phrase from her military training: *do not salute,* the drill sergeant had said, *if your head is empty.* And that, like locomotive, pulls along memories long sidetracked: of friendship that took all fear from the world, of camaraderie that shrunk to nothing the threat of flying bullets and exploding shells, of love that warmed even trench mud, even Baltic winter. Of being chosen -- trusted -- to guard the newborn Provisional Government of an infant republic.

Of celebrating today, November 7 New Style, her failure, that Julian October day, to do her duty.

The soldiers sheathe their sabers; the officer canters ahead, toward the train station. Trotsky smiles. Her husband bends toward her.

"It isn't a secret any more, so I can tell you," he says. "Poland has given the right of passage. These men will be in Brest-Litovsk by morning, on the German border two days after that. In Weimar, probably in a week."

The next group enters the viewing square: women, in workmen's faded blue - skirts, blouses, kerchiefs. They must be cold: in their bare hands they carry banners - "Long Live Permanent Revolution," "Glory to Red October." The music changes: it is now the famous "We bravely march to battle/To die as one for the power of the Soviets."

She draws a breath as one particular face approaches.

Is this real, or her memory painting over reality's palimpsest? This face belongs elsewhere, elsewhen, much closer, a bit askew, eyes unfocused and gazing into hers, lips touching lips.

Katya.

More memories surface like links of anchor chain winding on the capstan, emerging from deep, cold, murky waters: memories of the day they faced an army of deserters in front of the Winter Palace, and surrendered. Of running from Red death squads; of volleys of gunfire in the distance, too regular to come from battle; of forgetting her name and taking another off a gravestone of a girl born on her birthday and buried soon after; of running, alone, leaving Katya behind.

Of looking, hungry-eyed, at a man biting a loaf of bread.

Of being invited to share it, and staying.

The present reasserts itself. The woman's - Katya's? - eyes still look ahead; there is no change in her expression, her posture, the cadence of her steps. She banishes the thought of asking after her: death warrants for each surviving veteran of First Petrograd Women's Strike Battalion are still in effect. They, and rewards to informants, were announced within a week of Trotsky's accession.

A burning spark of cold pierces her cheek. She wipes away a tear; it freezes into a diamond on her glove. Her husband pats her shoulder. "Excellent," he whispers.

Parade lasts until dusk. More workers pass, and peasants herded in from nearby villages. It is November dark when her husband's Party limousine stops in front of their home. Their chauffeur leans on the horn; their servant opens the door. They enter the warmth that is still far too cold.

"Darling?" her husband says. "Comrade Trotsky was quite taken with you today. He said of all the people, your joy at this momentous celebration was most palpably sincere."

"He saw that?" she says and lifts her head.

"Comrade Trotsky sees everything," he says, and wipes her cheek, and a moment later his own.

Est Omnis Divisa

On the clay tablet, words, in that curious Cumaean
script, inverted lambdas and lopsided pi's, leaning left,
written left-handed:
"To prove
My love, give me a mountain to move,
A land to conquer, army to defeat
and lay the treasures of the world before your feet."
The dancing fire falls upon the face of that strange
boy the other refugees call "Little Janus:" the fossa in
the middle of his forehead where a stone had struck
him--from a Republican sling, or Tarquinist? Does it
matter?--the right side of his face contorted in sadness
and regret, the left still snarling in anger--left hand
stretched forward in supplication--bloody right hand
restrained by King's own bodyguard.

Another boy, dead on the frozen ground, half
firelit, half in the shadow cast by the brazier's base.

"Oh, Gaius," says the King. "Oh, Gaius."

"He came to bring you these," the bodyguard says.
"Flavius said that you are sleeping and not to be
disturbed. Gaius produced a dagger--"

"Enough," says the King. Everything blurs. In
silence everyone waits for his decision.

Pro: Gaius is a murderer.

Con: His mind is addled. His left hand writes
beautiful poems; each time he sees the King, the right

side of his face--curious, this--melts in--what the King had, until now, called admiration. His right hand clenches in wrath more often than not, the left side of the face constricted in a perpetual scowl.

Pro: Gaius is a murderer.

If only one could execute half a man.

"What have you to say for yourself?" says the King, a rhetorical question, for Gaius rarely speaks, and then only the simplest things, perhaps only the things on which his two halves agree, of which there aren't many. The King's voice cracks; tears blur his eyes. Now my mind is also split in two, he thinks, and catches his own face in a half-smile.

He lets the silence stretch. Each moment is a moment with Gaius alive; there will be many later with him dead.

Pro: Gaius is a murderer.

The camp is still; there is the crackling of the brazier, muted breathing of the gathered guards, whisper of the wind in the crowns of umbrella pines.

"Let go of him," says the King. There is a sound of shuffling feet, and then a deeper quiet. Wind ruffles the King's beard, tickles his nose with--

--the aroma of roasted meat?

Who cooks at midnight?

The King blinks back and swallows his tears. In front of him, pale faces, four mouths gaping in astonishment, one mouth closed, jaws clenched in pain.

Gaius. He stands at parade rest, right hand thrust into the fire. As the King watches, Gaius' skin splits, blood sizzles on the embers, the smell of burnt flesh rises, gags him. The King steps back involuntarily; Gaius keeps his place, his gaze locked with the King's like gladii in combat, and in a flash of clarity the King sees the solution in Gaius' face.

"Enough," he says. "Gaius, enough."

Gaius pulls back his hand, not too quickly. The King sees nods of admiration in the surrounding guards.

"Go to the City, Gaius," says the King.

In Gaius' face, the pain moves fractionally aside to let astonishment peer through: "Sire?" Gaius says.

"Go to Rome, Gaius," says the King.

He lets the silence linger until the burnt flesh smell dissipates. His thoughts line up like soldiers, ready for their marching orders.

"Like you, the City is injured; like you, split in half," he says.

He considers the near-symmetry of Gaius' face, something he had never seen before.

"If there is to be peace, the citizens must see this," the King continues. "Perhaps if they can look at you and see themselves reflected--"

"I deserve death," Gaius says, with ease the King had never heard in his voice before. It is a thing on which his two sides are in complete agreement.

"And you shall have it," the King says. "As shall we all, when gods so declare. Fortunate few die having accomplished some good for which they may be remembered. If you succeed, I doubt they will remember you as Little Janus. Your better hand has always been your left; let that henceforth be your cognomen. Go, save your City, Gaius Mucius Scaevola. Go."

Guards part. Slowly Gaius raises the ruin of his hand toward the King; there are no fingers to make certain of his intent, but the King chooses to see it as an acclamation. "Ave, Rex," Gaius says, turns on his heel, and fades into the darkness.

"I'd never question the King's decision," says a guard. "I only beg enlightenment--"

"Why?" the King says. "You may think it strange, but... never till now have I seen his face as one, never saw Gaius as a persona. Never saw him react to anything as one man."

"And now, Sire?"

"Pain," says the King. "Pain," he repeats, staring at dead Flavius at his feet. "Pain makes him whole," he whispers at Gaius' back, watching him stagger up the Aventine toward the cluster of hovels that is Rome.

Ghost Nutrients

Lipids

1970s

"Can I have some ice cream, Mom?" I ask. Mom's gaze flicks at my waist and back to my eyes. "Sure, if you want to," she says. "But think of your weight" rings in my ears ... something she had said yesterday.

And now I don't feel like having ice cream.

2020s

I pass the ice cream aisle without a second glance. Let her ghost enjoy it fully. Bon appetit, Mom's ghost.

Proteins

1970s

The bread is like nothing I've seen. Salami, ham — the kind you don't find in regular stores. At home we only ever put a single layer of cold cuts on our bread, and I've never seen anything like this. The other guests are piling their sandwiches as high as they can open their mouths, but I hesitate. I meet my mother's eyes and she whispers, "don't get used to this."

I put two layers on my sandwich: one transparent slice of ham and one of wine-colored salami.

2020s

I make my sandwich to take to work with me, with just a few slices of ham, one of low calorie cheese, and a pickle. You can have the rest, Mom's ghost.

Carbohydrates

1970's

There's an open box of chocolate on the table as I come home from school.

"Hi Mom!" I say. "What's the occasion?"

"Your report card is due, isn't it?"

"Yes," I say, dreading what is to follow.

"Do you have it?"

"Yes." I reach for it to show Mom.

"I don't need to see it. Just tell me if you think you earned this chocolate."

There is a B in my report. "I don't know," I whisper. It's mostly A's, but I see the A's like the cloth and the B like that hole in my pants I ripped in first grade, that Mom patched, that other kids teased me about all semester.

"At least you're honest about it."

The chocolate goes back untouched.

2020s

My wife leans in against my back.

"What have I done to earn --"

She shakes her head. "You looked like you needed a hug."

I twist in her embrace and put my arms around her.

Mom's ghost will have to go hungry for now.

Upon Reflection

It rains often in November in the region of Lazio, in the city of Roma, on Piazza del Colosseo. Souvenir vendors make little profit in the rain, and most withdraw to the shelter of coffee shops that line Via del Cardello and Via dei Frangipani, but of one man, a brown-skinned newcomer whose name no one knew, it was known that he never left his spot just off the Arch of Constantine, regardless of how cold the wind and how heavy the downpour. He sold, like everyone else, small ashtray replicas of the Colosseum, and unlike his colleagues, did not seem to have a long patter memorized, answering tourists in apparent monosyllables, but it did not escape anyone's attention that he appeared to conduct a brisk if unhurried trade. It was whispered about that had he ever been seen outside the very well-lit piazza traveled by carabinieri at all hours of day and night, he might find himself somewhat the worse for wear, but that was never more than idle speculation.

After a day or two, his nearest neighbor noticed a pattern. Each tourist who stopped at the newcomer's spot would point to a colosseum and ask, presumably, its cost. The tourist would grow still for a moment, then look up, then pay without haggling. The neighbor shared this with one of the friendlier carabinieri.

"Oh yes," the carabiniere said. "I have heard him. It was on a clear night, but the ashtrays were still full of water, and he said, 'The piece is free, but it's ten euro for the moon reflected in it,' and of course..."

The neighbor swore to himself and poured his entire supply of drinking water into his Colosseo ashtrays, and it being daytime sold more than a few clouds before a sudden squall drove him indoors.

It's colder in December, and nearly as rainy, but holidays being what they are, the vendors multiply off Via Salvi and Via da Feltre in expectation of Christmas crowds, and now all of them kept water in their Colossei and sold reflections of the Sun, moon, stars, or the blue of the Roman sky, but it was still only the newcomer with whom no one ever haggled, and at whose words the tourists froze each and every time, and such was the oddity of him that no one was greatly surprised when on the day of winter solstice a shimmering sphere formed around him, shrunk, and was gone, leaving behind only the ragged blanket lined with the little Colossei.

There was, of course, the obligatory investigation, the friendly carabiniere having grown less friendly in asking pointed questions, looking for inconsistencies in the stories the vendors told that would point to the one or several who conspired to remove an inconvenient competitor, but the stories matched, such as they were, and no one wanted to scare away tourists, so it was dropped. The neighbor moved a meter and a half to occupy the vacant spot, but even that did not improve his business much. On Christmas eve, two days after the disappearance, a tourist from New Jersey who spoke passable Napolitano and who had heard the rumor asked him about it.

The neighbor thought about it, looking around at the gathering crowds: Americans, Brits, Germans, French, Belgians milled about, craning their necks at the Arch and at the Coliseo. He sighed and spat on the grass.

"He could have sold a lot of ashtrays," he said to the tourist and added: "Ten euro each, you want?"

Virror, Virror

She blinked three times to boot her contacts, and braced herself for her double vision to clear, the real and the virtual images to coalesce, but the lag was a fraction of a second this time, much less disorienting than before.

"Oh, I love this new upgrade!" she said and watched him stagger momentarily as he booted his own. He looked like a sailor on a ship in a storm, she thought, and playfully willed him a pirate hat and an eye patch and a beard, erected a virror, and chuckled as he did a double take at their reflections.

"Arrgh," he said. "Shiver me lumbers!"

She laughed out loud then, still unfiltered and in street clothes. He loved her laugh, and her face when she laughed. The memory warmed her, as did his answering smile. The beard, she thought, creased very realistically, and rakishly. Perhaps he'd keep it in the mask he's wear shortly.

"I can't wait to see what you have in mind," she said. "You must have spent a fortune on my rig. Perfect real time masks, wow. Who are we, this time?"

Last masks and chill they had been Anthony and Cleopatra in Tutankhamen's burial chamber; the time before, Jane and Tarzan in Hagia Sofia.

"I've something different in mind," he said. "Shall we undress?"

"I can't wait," she said, her blush deepening. She willed the room to darken, in meatspace as well as in virtual, and shed her clothes in the privacy that gave her, trusting him not to switch to low-light vision. She heard his belt clink against the floor, and softer noises he made; she smelled his shampoo on a tiny gust of wind, most probably as he took off his shirt. She smiled, again, in the darkness.

She willed the lights to brighten slowly. "I'm ready," she said, turned to the mirror, and gasped.

In twilight, two naked people stood in front of the virror. Part of her mind admired the detail of the seamless, hi-res masks they wore, that moved without a perceptible lag, that were both unmistakably them and unmistakably old, sagging in all the places she was afraid she'd sag, wrinkling along her smile lines and frown lines and lines she did not know she had but that were clearly hers, her mask's hair gray and sparse; his own unsparing masks, potbelly and jowls and all --

"Oh my," she said.

The brightening light revealed in ever-sharpening detail their imperfect bodies: age spots, stretch marks, hair they had always taken care to remove. She moved, instinctively, to cover herself, and her mask's breasts swung in pendulous arcs. The room around them appeared faded too. Literally faded; wallpaper yellowed, printed flowers wilted, stains appeared on upholstery, cobwebs on the ceiling. She looked down, and the clothes on the floor appeared patched and wrinkled, too.

She looked at him, and met his gaze. Neither looked away. Not for a long time.

"Marry me?" he said.

She willed the masks to drop, showing him what she wanted him to see: not her real, younger, prettier face; not her real, athletic body; but her real, flowing, tears.

Not to Praise Her

I have some words to say. Some will be new to you, loanwords from *her* language. Attend, I shall endeavor to explain.

She was my adversary.

She was my friend.

She is *dead*.

"She" is a pronoun that refers to egg-carriers; also possessive "her," noun "woman" and adjective "female." There are other accommodations their language makes to indicate whether an individual is currently an egg-carrier or an inseminator.

"Dead" is our word, but one we rarely use. Her people deny regeneration; they see each interruption as we see the dying of a star; they fear it as we fear the heat death of the Universe.

Our people are genetically the same, separated by perhaps a thousand years of divergence. We're cross-fertile with them: a fact I have not ascertained in person. Yet the confusion in which they live, about the permanent and the fleeting, is as alien to us as their physiology is familiar. The trivial, ephemeral role we play in the process of regeneration is for them enshrined in their very grammar, said role being the first fact one learns from their personal pronouns – –

"Do you remember living," she said once, "before your last regeneration?"

"No," I said. "Do you remember learning to walk?"

She lowered her head. "Point taken," she said. "Do you at least know who you were?"

"I was decanted from my Shipwomb as Segment 9291125. My designator factors into three primes. In me, Segments 5, 239, and 311 continue."

"What if the counter is in error?" she said. "What if your designator is prime itself?"

"Then I continue the First Prime life," I said. "It does not matter. All lives are precious."

"And your aggression against us?"

She had fought like no one I had ever seen in her singleship against the squadron I commanded. When we disabled her craft, I boarded it certain to find its pilot interrupted. She was not; she fought my officers, tooth and claw, two of them damaged slightly, one to interruption. We put left her in a holding cell for three cycles. When we returned to remove her cadaver, we found her weakened by hunger and thirst, but once again she went for our throats, this time inflicting no damage. I have never seen anyone suffer as she did, and choose to suffer more.

"Our shipwombs here will stop when our star dies, less than a billion years from now," I said. "We must build shipwombs everywhere, then we can hold out till heat death of the Universe."

She told me they respect us because we're not afraid to die, and envy our faith in regeneration. I told her we're not afraid because we do not die, and faith is of no relevance. Time-space tensor calculations work the same regardless of belief in infinitesimals, do they not? It is the same with our segmented lives. In early parts of our segments when we learn necessary skills in life resumption schools, we undergo supervised near-interruptions. They are unpleasant enough to keep us from self-interrupting for trivial reasons, but not nearly so to be feared as we fear pain, debility, or, worst of all, extinction.

This segment of my life has gone uninterrupted longer than any in our history. I'm almost deaf and blind. It hurts to walk. She asked me if we have substances that ease discomforts. Except for me, who'd need them? I've longed for interruption longer than you've been alive, but I delayed for these important reasons.

I wished to study her.

She feared death, this interruption without regeneration. She thought us braver than her people for not sharing this fear. She thought her people weaker for they mourn, they use extraordinary means to extend damaged segments, they mark their dead with funerals, for they are gone forever. And yet they fight. Through fear, through pain, through shame, through pains not one of us would suffer uninterrupted, yes, through lives such as mine has now become.

It is in part by my efforts that our war is interrupted, but this is not enough. I fear attacking her people again will be the last mistake our people make. I fear this war will wipe out all of us, every egg-carrier, every inseminator, every shipwomb. I fear there being no more regeneration.

This war must not regenerate. You must remember this. When I am interrupted, upon regeneration this is the first thing I must learn in life resumption school:

This war must die, as she has died.

Peace

If only you could see her face.

She is the angel of peace. She is the whore of the battlefield. She is the object of desire of some, the target of the ire of others. She avoids them all.

The war that came to her home was the least photogenic war of all: there was another that produced more picturesque orphans, another with far more entertaining dirges. Her war had been forgotten, until she took upon herself the task of fluffing it.

Each day she trained her camera upon the sky beyond, upon the strafing planes and the exploding shells. With battle for her backdrop, she filmed herself make love to soldiers, couples, widows and widowers, old people mourning their sons and daughters, young people in fear of bombs and press-gangs and deserters.

She made her war the most watched, most followed, highest rated war ever. She was the princess of the air, the queen of the digital screen, the marquess of the moving image. She had no rival.

Three other wars fizzled and died for lack of interest while her campaign went on; a few wars fizzled out before they fairly started. But her own war went on and on. To be sure, the casualties fell among civilians, for no one wanted to look sloppy and careless while sharing her spotlight; but many of those saved from random explosions were later drafted and killed by well-aimed fire. The highest-rated videos, in fact, were those of her making love to people who later died.

She quit, much later than anyone expected, but within hours others – men and women – sprung up to take her place. She hides now, in a place where plain black cloaks and covered faces are commonplace. She brought peace to so much of the world; so much, but not to the people of her homeland.

Between the advertising revenue and the tourist trade, they can't afford peace now.

Made in the USA
Columbia, SC
28 February 2022

56964695R00148